Twisted Cross Ranch Book One

sinner's
secret

K. Loraine
USA Today Bestselling Authors
Meg Anne

This book is a work of fiction. The names, characters, places, and incidents are products of the author's imagination or have been used fictitiously and are not to be construed as real. Any resemblance to persons, living or dead, actual events, locales, or organizations is entirely coincidental.

Copyright 2023 © Ravenscroft Press

All rights reserved.

ISBN:

978-1-961742-00-0 (Paperback Edition)

978-1-961742-01-7 (Hardback Edition)

You may not copy, distribute, transmit, reproduce, or otherwise make available this publication (or any part of it) in any form, or by any means (including without limitation electronic, digital, optical, mechanical, photocopying, printing, recording, or otherwise), without the prior written permission of the author.

Permission requests can be sent via email to: authors@themategames.com

Edited by Mo Sytsma of Comma Sutra Editorial

Cover Design by T.E. Black Designs

Photographer: Wander Aguiar

Model: Michael M.

To Wrangler jeans.
You know what you did, and we sure appreciate you for it. Thank you for decades of eye candy.

"A man who puts a hand on a member of my family never puts a hand on anything else."

— Jamie Dutton, Yellowstone

sinner's secret

K. LORAINE
USA TODAY BESTSELLING AUTHORS
MEG ANNE

authors' note

Sinner's Secret contains mature and graphic content which may be triggering for some readers. Such content includes scenes of breeding kink, hand necklaces, assault, gore, torture, murder, and more. **Reader discretion is advised.**

As always, a detailed list of content and trigger warnings is available on our website.

one

River

People say you should face your demons. Clearly, they've never had to stand on the devil's doorstep. Daniel Cross Jr. was my own personal demon, and I'd happily left him behind a decade ago, promising myself I'd never come back to Twisted Cross Ranch.

Unfortunately fate had other plans.

I glanced warily at the overnight bag I'd refused to let out of my sight. A shudder worked its way down my spine that had nothing to do with the AC blasting in the ostentatious black Land Rover and everything to do with apprehension. I gripped my hands tighter, knotting my fingers together until I could barely feel them, and forced myself to look back out the window at the sprawling monstrosity that was the lodge.

"Look, ma'am, I'm paid by the hour, so you can sit in this car all you want, but I'd rather drive us somewhere else if that's the case." The driver's eyes found mine in the rearview mirror. He didn't like it here either. Smart man.

"No. I'm getting out. I just . . . it's been a long time."

As he climbed out of the car, he made a soft sound in his throat that could have been understanding or judgment. It was hard to tell in the south. Everything was layered beneath a facade of genteel manners and an ever-present threat of danger. Southern gentlemen were everything they promised to be, but the question was, were they promising to ruin you or rescue you?

The driver opened my door, holding out a hand to help me down from the tall SUV. My heart caught in my throat as soon as the familiar scents of the ranch hit me. Memories I didn't want to relive flooded my mind, sending a panic response through my veins. Daniel Cross Sr.—known simply as 'Senior' to those of us close to him—might be dead and gone, but his legacy had clearly been upheld. Twisted Cross hadn't changed a bit in ten years. The place that used to sit at the heart of my best childhood moments should have been a welcome sight. Instead, a wave of nausea accompanied my approach.

"I'll take your bag," the driver offered, but I held fast, not willing to part with my belongings.

"No. I've got it."

"Are you gonna be okay, miss? You're white as a sheet."

"I'm fine." I offered him a tight smile that I knew he didn't buy any more than I did.

With a tip of his hat, he left me to make the short walk alone.

The shadow of the house loomed over me, and another shiver racked my frame. I blamed my dress just to have something other than my thoughts to blame for the unconscious reaction. Running my free hand over the flared skirt of the simple black frock I'd purchased specifically for my grand return, I resisted the urge to adjust my silver belt for the millionth time. I could have gone full-on siren in a body-hugging sheath that showed off my curves, but instead I chose something appropriate for the somber occasion while still being flattering and demure. Something comfortable enough for the tomboy in me that would show everyone I was put together and mature without screaming for their attention. Neither of the Cross boys deserved to see me in that light. Least of all Daniel.

The door flew open, startling me out of my mini pep talk. A squeak of fright left me, and the breath I hadn't realized I was holding whooshed out when I realized the man in the doorway was not the Cross brother I feared.

"Walker?" I asked, not quite sure the tall, heavily tattooed man in front of me was the boy I once knew. Not until those familiar blue eyes landed on me and he offered me a lopsided grin. He'd changed. A lot. Walker Cross had been my best friend on this ranch when we were growing up. We'd spent nearly as much time here as at my own house until the day after I turned eighteen.

But that gangly boy with his freckled face and gap-toothed smile was nowhere to be found on the sexy as sin, rugged, stubbled man giving me a very thorough once-over. "River Adams, as I live and breathe. Is that really you?"

"It is. I . . . who the hell did you turn into? You're all broad and muscly. You were so worried you'd never fill out." I reached out and squeezed his bulging bicep. "Guess you were wrong."

He gave me a cocky wink and flexed until the material of his western-style shirt threatened to bust. "Trust me, darlin', it took a lot of work."

"Don't you dare darlin' me."

"Sweetcheeks?"

"No."

"Sugartits?"

"Wow. I bet you're still single, aren't you?"

"Only by choice, sweetheart. The ladies love me."

"Buckle bunnies, you mean?"

"There's that accent, guess you haven't lost it completely after all."

I knew my southern drawl had faded over the years, only

popping out when riled up or well in my cups, but I hadn't realized it would come back so quickly.

Walker's smile stretched as he crossed his arms and leaned against the doorframe. "But I don't remember you being so judgmental. There was a time I recall you were right there lusting for cowboys alongside them."

My cheeks burned. "I was a misguided youth. I'm much more into lumberjacks now."

"Oh yeah?"

"Yeah. I've got a thing for flannel."

He shook his head and chuckled before righting himself and pulling me in for a bear hug. "It's really great to see you, ladybug."

Hearing the nickname he'd used for me growing up eased a little of the stress I'd been carrying due to this visit.

"Is Cross here?" I managed to get out after he put me down and offered me his arm. Grateful for the guidance, I took it and let him lead me through the sprawling house.

"Yeah. Of course he's here. Grumpy asshole is always here, especially now that Dad's gone. I won't be surprised if he just moves into the office and mounts his name on the damn door."

I winced. There was very little love lost between the brothers. Always had been. I didn't understand it when I was young, not until the rumors about Walker finally reached my ears. The Cross boys notoriously had a very strong family resemblance. All but the youngest. Walker's hair was a few shades too dark, his eyes a few too light. People speculated he might actually be the product of their mom having a tryst with some long-forgotten ranch hand. And gossip in a town like this spread like wildfire. Hot and fast.

"I'm so sorry to hear about your dad, Walker. I really am, but I have no idea why I was summoned here. I'm not family."

It felt good to finally get that off my chest. When I'd gotten the call telling me Senior had died, I'd been shocked to learn my presence was requested at the reading of his will. Dread followed and never left the pit of my stomach.

Walker scrubbed a hand along his jaw. "Me neither, ladybug. It was a shock when we saw your name on the list. Selfishly, I'm glad you're here, though. It's been too long. You forget how phones work or something?" Some of the playfulness left him as he admitted, "I waited for you, you know. In our spot. Didn't think you'd actually take off without saying goodbye or leaving a note . . ."

It was clear he was waiting for an explanation. One I couldn't give him.

Swallowing past the lump in my throat, I searched for some way to convey my promise to my parents without hurting him. When I left, it had been in the dead of night, with nothing more than a bag of clothes and enough money to get me on a bus going far away from this town. I'd sworn to him I'd never come back. Never see the Cross family again. But that was before my parents were killed. Before Senior died. And most of all, before I'd received the letter burning a hole in my bag.

"It's complicated."

The lighthearted warmth evaporated from his tone as I brushed him off. "Fine. Keep your secrets. Everyone's waiting in here."

Wiping clammy palms on my skirt, I shored up every ounce of courage I had as he slid open the two large pocket doors to reveal the last man on earth I wanted to see.

Daniel Cross Jr. stood with his back to me, but I knew it was him the instant my eyes landed on that towering form. As if he could feel my gaze, he slowly spun around and pinned me with fathomless midnight-blue eyes.

I was ten years old the first time a horse threw me. It had been on this very ranch, with Cross as my teacher. I'd thought I was dying because my lungs wouldn't work; all the air had been punched out of them from the impact with the ground. He'd stood over me, those blues focused on me as I struggled and finally drew breath. That's how this felt. Like I was suffocating under his stare. Lost and desperate for him to let me breathe again.

It had always been like that when I found myself on the receiving end of Cross's undivided attention. In my years pretending he didn't exist, I'd forgotten how wholly he could control me with a single look. He was a black hole sucking me in with his gravitational pull, and I was, as always, helpless to stay out of his orbit.

Walker's palm on the small of my back startled me out of the Cross spiral I'd been trapped in. "Danny, you remember River, don't you?"

Cross's expression didn't change, but the temperature in the room noticeably dropped as he managed to turn my name into a curse with a single growled word.

"River."

Ten years earlier

"WHAT IS THIS AGAIN?" I asked my dad as I put pen to paper.

"Just some financial documents," he said evasively. "Nothing to worry about. Your mama and I just want to make sure you're looked after if anything happens."

I frowned at him, looking up as I hastily scrawled my name on the dotted line, ready to protest the possibility, but he stopped me with a kiss on the top of my head.

"Go get back to your party, sweetpea. I can't believe

you're already eighteen. It seems like you were knee high to a bug's eye just yesterday."

Now I was rolling my eyes as I adjusted the neckline of the white taffeta gown Mama had picked out for me especially for this party. "Why is it you always get more southern the more you drink?" I asked, giving his nearly empty highball glass a suspicious poke.

"Whiskey precedes wisdom," he intoned before winking. "Now, get."

I scampered off toward the crowd made up of my parents' friends. For a birthday party, this didn't feel like it was about me at all. I was just a means to an end, an excuse for them to celebrate. But the multitude of cash-filled envelopes on the gift table would at least all go to me. I guess it wasn't all bad.

I bit my lip, trying to see where Walker had run off to. He'd had a crush on Daisy Stewart all summer and told me tonight was the night he was finally going to get under her skirt. He'd had a growth spurt, and she finally seemed interested in returning his longing looks. Poor guy. Always in Cross's shadow. But how could he not be when his older brother looked like *that*.

A little curl of heat licked through my belly, same as it always did when I thought about Daniel Cross Jr. He was the epitome of everything I wanted in a man. Because that's exactly what he was. A man with a capital M. He'd always been more serious, his dark, moody eyes lacking the laugh lines around them that his brother had. I was pretty sure he came out of the womb with muscles and the thick stubble that had always coated his square jaw. I wanted to run my fingers over the scruff and see what it felt like. To finally know what it would feel like to be wrapped up in his arms, his lips inches away from mine. To let my fingers dive into his dark honey hair and finally find out if it was as silky as it looked while his delicious fresh grass, warm tobacco, and leather scent surrounded me. *Yes, I've spent a lot of time thinking of this and yes, I might have stolen a shirt or two of his over the years.*

He had no idea I existed, of course. Not beyond the fact that I was a constant nuisance, just like his little brother. But tonight, everything was about to change. I was a woman now. An adult who could take the bull by the horns and make him hers.

The man in question caught my eye as he slunk away from the house. Not about to let him get away, I grabbed a flute of champagne from a nearby waiter and downed it in one, proud of myself for only wincing a little as the bubbles burned up my throat. Then, remembering my father's words, I grabbed a glass of whiskey for good measure. That didn't go down quite as easy, and I was thankful no one was paying any attention as I sputtered and gagged.

Real sexy, River. It's no wonder the boys don't come a runnin'.

After a steadying breath and yet another tug on the neckline of my gown, I snatched one more champagne flute and slipped out of the house and into the warm summer night. I knew exactly where he was headed. The same place Cross always went when he wanted to be alone. The gazebo. My favorite place in the world. He didn't know that, of course. Sometimes I wasn't even sure he remembered my name. All he'd called me was 'sparrow' since I turned ten.

With its fairy lights and the gentle babble of the nearby stream and little pond, the gazebo had always seemed magical to me. I couldn't think of a better place to make Cross mine. Especially when the stars were out like they were tonight, big and bright in the clear sky. It was like a sign from above. Tonight was the night.

I felt warm all over, but couldn't say for sure whether it was from the alcohol or excitement. Either way, I was near breathless by the time I caught up to him. Good God, he was beautiful. He stood there, leaning against a post, hat tipped low, hiding most of his face and perfecting the broody romantic hero look he was so good at. He'd dressed up too, , maybe his daddy'd forced it on him just like my mama had? Polished black boots, dark jeans, and a black blazer, with his nicest Stetson too. You'd think he was attending a wedding, not a birthday party. It made me smile to know he was wearing this for me.

He brought a joint to his lips, sucking in the smoke and holding it for a few seconds before releasing the pungent cloud on a sigh.

"You know, smoking's bad for you, right?" I teased, coming into the gazebo without asking permission.

He glanced over his shoulder at me and purposefully took another hit. "Sweet girl like you should probably go back inside with Mommy and Daddy, then."

"I'm not so sweet."

"Is that so, sparrow?"

"Uh huh." I snatched the joint from between his fingers and brought it to my lips. I'd never smoked weed. Not once. But he didn't need to know that.

His brows lifted as he waited, calling my bluff. I sucked in a breath, the smoke burning and instantly making my eyes water as I coughed.

Lips twitching in a half smile, he shook his head and reclaimed his joint. "Yeah, you're a real outlaw."

If I could just stop coughing, I'd show him. But my head swam, and I nearly gagged. That would be just great. I'd really make him see that the eight years between us didn't matter anymore if I puked all over his boots. So, I made my way to the railing and braced my hands on the wood as I pulled it together. Like a lady.

Eventually a warm palm rested between my shoulder blades, and his deep gravelly voice crooned in my ear, "Slow breaths, sparrow. Then just ride out the high."

"I'm . . . fine."

A low, rumbled laugh was his only response as I brought

my champagne to my lips and choked it down. Once the spasms in my chest stopped, I turned toward him.

He was a lot closer than I realized, and my move put us in what my friend Addie called 'kissing distance'. My breath caught as he lifted his hand and used his thumb to brush away a tear that slipped down my cheek.

"You'll ruin your pretty makeup," he murmured, gaze locked on my lips.

No one had ever used the words pretty and me in the same sentence before. Besides my daddy. I was a tomboy through and through. Which is part of the reason Mama had to force me into this dress. I preferred jeans and boots to skirts and sandals. But right now, with the way Cross was looking down at me, I was having a change of heart.

He made me feel special. Delicate. Something I'd never experienced since I always towered over the boys my own age. But Cross was a head taller than me, his shoulders wide and chest heavily muscled. Everything about him was big, from his frame to his presence. And he'd never touched me. Not like this. Not with tenderness and affection.

His fingers slid down the column of my throat until they trailed along my exposed collarbone.

This was it. My big moment.

"It's my birthday, you know," I blurted. *Smooth, River. Real smooth.*

His eyes twinkled with laughter. "Yeah, I'm aware."

"I think that means you owe me a present."

His brow kicked up. "A present?"

I licked my lips and nodded. "Uh huh. And I know exactly what I want."

"And what would that be?"

You.

My belly fluttered as I leaned in a little closer. "A kiss."

I don't know where the bravado came from. I was trembling, and my heart was beating so hard I was afraid he would be able to hear it. But I could tell I'd surprised him. He went super still, his eyes dropping to my lips and lingering there before returning to my eyes.

"Sparrow . . ."

I didn't think I could survive his rejection, so I didn't give him a chance to finish letting me down gently. Instead, I reached up and took his face in my hands and clumsily slammed my lips against his.

I expected him to push me away, to tell me we couldn't do this, that I was just a silly little girl with a crush. But he didn't do any of those things. Instead, he let out a pained groan and threaded his fingers through my hair, tangling in the long wavy strands as he tugged my head back and deepened the kiss.

That sound he made would live rent-free in my head as long as I lived.

Kissing Cross was everything I'd ever dreamed and more. My imagination couldn't have predicted the scrape of his beard against my skin or the heat of his smoke and whiskey breath fanning my lips and sliding against my tongue. He tasted like midnight promises and forevers. Daniel Cross Jr. was going to ruin me for all men, and I was ready to let him.

He broke the kiss, breaths coming in heavy pants as he stared down at me. I didn't want him to let go of me.

Running his thumb over my bottom lip, he asked, "Was that your first kiss, sparrow?"

Fear pierced the happy little bubble I'd been living in. Shit. What had been the single most important moment of my life must have sucked for him, thanks to my inexperience. "Uh . . ."

"Don't lie to me."

Somehow I didn't think he was referring to the awkward kissing session Walker and I had participated in right before the start of ninth grade. That had been two best friends trying to figure out the particulars of what to do with their noses. Nothing like this.

"It's the first one that counts."

His hold on my face tightened just enough to catch my attention. "What's that supposed to mean?"

"It was nothing. Kid stuff."

His eyes narrowed. "Who got to you first?"

I swallowed, worried I was about to ruin everything. "Walker."

He looked away, breathing deep through his nose before asking, "You want him?"

Shaking my head, I whispered, "No. It's you, Cross. It's always been you."

He speared me with his gaze, stealing every ounce of air in my lungs. "You're damn right it is." Dipping his head, he claimed my lips again, backing me up until he could lift me onto the banister and ruck up my skirt so he could fit his hips between my spread legs.

When he rocked into me, I moaned, thousands of fireworks lighting up beneath my skin. It had never felt this good when I'd touched myself, and all he'd done was brush his body against mine.

I was shivering and aching for something I couldn't name as he ran his calloused palm up my thigh. His thumb swept low, dipping so close to where I wanted him to touch me.

"What about this?" he breathed against my lips. "Anyone else give you this?"

And then he *was* touching me, his fingers ghosting over my center and making me cry out.

"No one. No one but you and . . ."

The pad of his thumb ran across my panty-clad core, and I bucked in his hold, searching for more. "And?"

"Me. No one has touched me there except for when I do it myself."

"And who do you ache for when you make yourself come at night, in the quiet, under your covers, sparrow?"

"You, Cross. Always you."

"Fuck," he whispered. "If I was a better man, I'd stop this here and now. But I've always been a selfish asshole, and that's not gonna change anytime soon."

"Good. I don't want you to stop."

"You're too young."

"I'm eighteen."

He traced the line of my panties with his fingertip. "Believe me, I know."

"I want it to be you." When he still seemed like he might reconsider, I added, "Please, Cross?"

He closed his eyes, his nose brushing mine, but then his eyes snapped open, and he turned to look behind him. "Someone's coming."

"Then take me somewhere else. Somewhere we can be alone."

He groaned. "You're killing me, sparrow."

"And you're giving me everything I ever wanted."

Snagging the bottle of whiskey, he took a long pull before lifting me off the rail and murmuring, "Wrap your legs around me. I'm not letting you go until you're under me."

Those words in his deep rasp were almost enough to send me toppling over the edge. He was my every fantasy come to life, and he'd only just gotten started.

I think my brain short-circuited then, because I wasn't sure how we made the trip from the gazebo to the barn.

"Here?" I asked as he held the ladder to the loft steady.

"It's that or parade you through the house and risk getting caught by our parents."

I shuddered. No, thank you.

I climbed up to the loft we'd all used as our rec room over the last eighteen years. It was pretty cozy, all things considered. I grabbed and laid out a blanket while he climbed up behind me. I'd just added two pillows and was still kneeling beside my makeshift bed when he joined me.

Fathomless blue eyes held me captive as he took off his hat and placed it on the floor next to him.

"If you wanna stop, all you have to do is say the word. I'm not gonna force the issue or make you do anything you don't want, baby."

That, more than anything else, told me I was making the right decision. Cross was it for me. I would love him for the rest of my life, and there was no one else I trusted to give my virginity to.

"I want you. I'm not going to stop you."

I was trembling but trying desperately to hide it. The last thing Cross needed was to see me shaking like a leaf.

With slow, deliberate movements, he unbuttoned his shirt, then shrugged out of both his blazer and the crisp white button-down. Every slab of muscle was on display just for me, like my dream come true. His body was crafted from hard work on the ranch and long hours in the sun.

I reached for him, needing to touch him and remind myself that this was real. That I wasn't dreaming.

But he had something else in mind.

"Stand up, little sparrow." He held out his hand for me and helped me to my feet. When I thought he might kiss me again, he placed his hands on my hips and spun me around.

"What—"

But my words dried up when he gently brushed my hair off my neck and over my shoulder so he could unzip my dress. Goosebumps broke out along my skin as the dress fell to the floor, exposing my bare breasts and the soaked silk between my legs.

"Fucking perfect," he whispered, his lips feathering across my shoulder as he stepped into me, warm chest against my back.

His hands were unhurried as he slid them up my sides,

leaving more goosebumps in his wake. No one had ever touched me like this. Like they were savoring me. I may not have much to compare it to, but I knew the way Cross treated me was special. I moaned into his touch as he cupped my breasts with both palms, his thumbs brushing my sensitive nipples and sending shockwaves through me.

"You like that?" he rasped.

"Yes. Oh, yes. Please do it again."

He made a rumbling sound and did as I asked. I gave a little jerk, my butt pressing into his rock-hard erection. Realizing I was just standing here while he was doing all the work, I reached back, wanting to make him feel as good as I did.

Turning me to face him, he knelt in front of me and hooked his fingers in the waistband of my underwear. I would never forget his expression as he rolled his eyes up to silently ask for permission.

I bit my lip and nodded, giving a little squeak of surprise when he pressed his lips against my mound once I was bared to him.

"Lie back, sparrow. I wanna see you."

Oh God.

I'm sure there were a million other sexy ways to do this. Or maybe to give him back a little of what he was giving me, but I was so out of my depth I couldn't think of a single one. So I did as he said, trusting him to make this good for both of us.

There was no other word for the expression on his face besides reverent as he took his time raking his gaze over my body. I swear I could feel it as if his hands were traveling the same path.

"You are so fucking beautiful, River."

River. Not sparrow.

"I need you, Cross. Please."

"Soon, baby. I gotta get you ready for me. Your tight little pussy needs to open up if it's gonna take all of me."

"Oh," I breathed, so freaking turned on I couldn't manage more than that.

He pushed my thighs farther apart and then settled his shoulders between them. Instinct had me wanting to close my legs, but the second his breath hit me, that thought fled. Then all I wanted was more.

I cried out as his tongue slid across that special place I touched in the privacy of my own bed. He knew exactly where to touch me to make me feel good. My fingers went to his thick hair, and I held on to him as he licked and sucked, slipping one digit between my folds and making me moan as he toyed with my entrance. Glancing down my body, I shuddered in pleasure at the sight of his head between my legs, eyes focused on my face as he made me feel things I didn't know existed.

When he pressed his finger inside me, I stiffened at the intrusion, but then he curled it, and all I knew was bliss. He did it again, and my body shook, chasing whatever he was offering.

I'd made myself come plenty of times, but my orgasms were nothing compared to what he was building inside me. It was like comparing vanilla ice cream to a triple chocolate sundae. One was good. The other was in a whole different league.

He added a second finger and did that magical curling thing again as his tongue focused on the perfect spot. But it was his groan against my sensitive flesh that tipped me over the edge. I came, crying his name and tugging on his hair, thighs shaking so hard they hurt.

When he was done, he sat back on his heels and wiped his mouth with the back of his hand, a satisfied smirk on his lips. "Now you're ready."

He reached for the jeans he'd shucked off earlier, pulling a

Sinner's Secret

foil packet from his back pocket. I didn't know why that made me blush after he'd just had his face between my legs, but it did.

Holding my gaze, he tore the foil with his teeth and then slid the condom over his daunting length.

Again, I didn't have a lot to compare him to, but the few references I had were sorry compared to what Cross was packing. I was sure I'd never walk straight again.

"W-will it hurt?" I asked, hating the stammer in my words.

"It might. I'll go slow and do everything I can to make it feel good for you."

I nodded as he got into position between my legs.

"You still sure this is what you want, baby?"

Staring up at him poised at my center, eyes hooded with desire for me, there was only one answer to that question.

"I've never been more sure about anything in my life."

He pressed inside me, slow and smooth, and he was right—it did hurt until my body stretched and the pain turned to a different kind of pleasure. As we moved together, he loved me with his sweet words and soft lips, filling me with the certainty that Cross was meant for me. He was The One.

With a groan, he tensed, and I could tell he was coming, the sensation of him swelling and jerking inside me setting off another wave of toe-curling bliss inside me.

Breathing hard, he rested his forehead against mine, one arm bracketing my head while he trailed the fingers of the other hand gently down my cheek. I forced my eyes open, a dreamy smile on my lips as I stared up at him.

Our eyes locked and held, and my heart felt so full as I drowned in the gaze of the man who'd just irrevocably changed my life.

"I love you," I whispered, the words taking flight on their own. I couldn't have stopped them if I tried. In that moment, they were my absolute truth, and after what we'd just experienced together, I didn't want to pretend. Surely he could see it written on my face anyway.

But he didn't say it back like my foolish heart had hoped. Instead of love in his eyes, all I saw in response to my declaration was absolute terror.

two

Cross

Present day

"River."

The last time I saw River Adams, I was inside her, taking her virginity, making her mine as she told me she loved me.

Biggest fucking mistake of my life. Which was saying something, considering how I made my living.

Years of hurt and confusion burned in emerald eyes that always saw way too fucking much. I was an asshole, but I knew that and never pretended to be anything different. It was on her if she hadn't seen me for who I was. For a girl who watched me like a hawk, she'd been looking through rose-colored glasses where I was concerned.

"Is it cold in here, or is that just me?" Walker asked in a misguided attempt at lightening the mood.

Without acknowledging my brother's words, I cut a glance over to the lawyer standing at the head of our long conference table. My father had this made out of a slab from one of the red oaks surrounding the property that had fallen during a storm when I was a kid. It used to fascinate me to no end. I'd spend hours tracing the ragged edges of the wood, imagining the grooves were paths on a map of a fantastical world far away from here. That was before I'd been shown the bitter truths of reality.

Now, I didn't imagine a damn thing. There was no escaping my reality, and it was better for everyone if I remembered that. People had a way of finding themselves on the wrong side of a rifle when I forgot.

Or worse.

The Crosses weren't good people. We may have more money than God and a damn castle to boot, but we were the bad guys, and we did bad things. End of story.

I didn't need to say a word as I held McCreedy's stare. Years working side by side in our fathers' shadows had made us partners of a sort. Usually he was cleaning up my mess, but I paid him well for the privilege, so he didn't say shit when I told him to jump. He just fucking jumped. It's why we worked so well together. If a man like me had friends, McCreedy would be the closest thing I had.

The lawyer gave me a little nod and opened his briefcase while I pulled out a chair and sat as Walker and River took their places across from me.

"All right. Miss Adams, I'm Jackson McCreedy, the Cross family's attorney. Thank you for joining us. I know it was a long trip from Alaska." He pulled out three manila folders and passed one to each of us. "The stipulations of Cross Senior's will were very clear, and we wouldn't be able to do this today if you hadn't joined us in person."

River glanced around the room, her expression filled with confusion. "Is this everyone? I honestly don't understand why I'm part of this. I'm not family."

"No. You aren't," I grumbled, forcing myself to look into her eyes again, even though facing her was the last thing I wanted to do. To say I didn't want her here was a massive fucking understatement. If I had my way, she wouldn't be within a hundred miles of this place. "She shouldn't be here."

"It's not my place to know why, only to do," McCreedy said with a self-deprecating smile.

"Don't listen to my brother, ladybug. He's had a stick up his ass since the day you left town. I'm glad you're here. It's been too damn long." Walker took her hand and squeezed.

If I clenched my teeth any harder, my molars were going to fucking crack.

"The sooner we get this over with, the sooner she can go back to wherever the fuck she was hiding." I stared McCreedy down and opened my folder. "What the fuck is this?" I asked, my eyes lifting from what appeared to be a transcript.

"I was getting to that." McCreedy grabbed a remote and pushed a button, opening a panel on the wall and turning on a flat-screen TV.

My father's face appeared on the screen, and what felt like a thousand insects began to crawl beneath my skin. From the look of him, this had been made within the last year. His hair was peppered with gray, eyes sharp but sporting deep crow's feet, jaw unshaven with a neatly trimmed beard.

"Hello, boys. River. I'd say it's good to see y'all, but we all know that's not why you're watching this. My life caught up with me. I hope the funeral was nice." He glanced off camera and nodded. "Jackson says I need to get to the point, so here we go. I, Daniel Everett Cross Senior, being of sound mind and body, declare this my last will and testament." He held up a newspaper displaying the date—two months before his death—then continued. "This ain't gonna be an easy pill to swallow for any of you, but I have my reasons. To my eldest son, Daniel Everett Cross Junior, I leave my collection of antique guns, my horse Julep, and a twenty-five percent share of Twisted Cross Ranch, along with all related Cross Industries assets."

My gut clenched. Twenty-five percent? "Are you fucking serious?"

"To my son, Walker Wayne Cross, I leave my collection of classic cars with the stipulation that if one is totaled due to his negligence, ownership will immediately pass to Junior, and a twenty-five percent share of Twisted Cross Ranch, along with all related Cross Industries assets."

I couldn't believe this was happening. "This has to be a joke."

Anger burned in my brother's eyes. "No less than I expected," he muttered, used to my father's mind games.

On screen, my father sighed heavily. "Now this is the part I know will come as the biggest shock, but I want y'all to know, as I said before, I have my reasons, which hopefully will become clear in due time. So last, River Danielle Adams, I leave you the remaining fifty percent share of Twisted Cross Ranch, along with all related Cross Industries assets."

I jumped to my feet, slamming my hands on the table. "This is bullshit!"

McCreedy paused the video and waited silently.

My fiery gaze pinned River. "What did you do to him to get him to give you all this? Were the two of you fucking in secret? Couldn't keep the heir, so you went for the king instead?"

Her eyes widened, and a flush stained her cheeks, but she managed to keep her voice even as she said, "I may like older men, Cross, but not that much older, and as you already know, I've been in Alaska. So unless this supposed affair was a virtual one and my pussy is so magical, just looking at it is enough to inspire a man to acts of madness, your theory is dead in the water."

I happened to know for a fact how magical her pussy was,

and it only infuriated me further. "Who's to say you were even there? If it acts like a whore and looks like a whore—"

"That's enough, Cross," Walker growled, getting to his feet, ready to put himself between her and me. "Let's see what else the old man has to say. We can't change it."

"Maybe not, but if you think I won't be contesting this bullshit, you're dead fucking wrong." I stormed to the bar on the other side of the room, fuming as I went. Once I'd poured myself a liberal serving of whiskey, I took a deep breath, knocked it back, and nodded at McCreedy to continue. I needed to be as far away from River as possible.

The video resumed, and my asshole game-playing father grinned on the screen. "I know you're likely throwing a hissy fit right now, but it can't be helped. This is how it has to be. Half of this company was always her birthright, and with her father gone, it rightfully belongs to her. In addition to the majority shares of the ranch and all business interests, I'm leaving the lodge to River on the stipulation that both my boys get to stay. The rest of the details are in the document Jackson has prepared for you three." The old man lifted a glass of whiskey, tipped his hat, and winked at the camera before the screen went dark.

River sat there, her eyes wide, disbelief stamped on her face. It was almost enough to make me believe her innocent act wasn't all smoke and mirrors. Almost.

McCreedy cleared his throat. "That's not all, I'm afraid. If I could please direct your attention to the final page of the document I handed to you. It outlines the remaining pertinent details."

"You mean there's more?" River asked.

"Ladybug, when it comes to our father, there's always more. Senior isn't happy unless he's well and truly fucked you."

Shaking with anger, I returned to my seat and flipped to the last page of his transcript.

There it was, in bullet-pointed bold font.

- **RIVER DANIELLE ADAMS MUST MAINTAIN RESIDENCE AT TWISTED CROSS RANCH FOR A PERIOD OF NO LESS THAN 365 CONSECUTIVE DAYS PRIOR TO ANY SALE OR TRANSFER OF HER MAJORITY SHARES.**

- **THIS STIPULATION ALSO PERTAINS TO THE SALE OR TRANSFER OF ANY AND ALL PROPERTIES AND ASSETS OWNED BY TWISTED CROSS RANCH AND/OR CROSS INDUSTRIES.**

- **SHOULD MS. ADAMS VACATE THE PROPERTY, ALL SHARES WILL BE PLACED IN A TRUST ONLY ACCESSIBLE BY MCCREEDY AND SONS UNTIL SOLD AT PUBLIC AUCTION.**

MY FURY WAS ALL-CONSUMING. There was no goddamn universe in which I would be okay with River Adams becoming my roommate. Fuck, not just my roommate, my damn landlord. The property was more than big enough for us to never cross paths, but I wasn't fool enough to believe that would actually happen. If she was here, constantly underfoot, I'd find her. Just like when she was a kid. She'd always been a moth, and I was the flame, ready to burn off her wings. Or maybe I was fooling myself, and it was the other way around.

"But I don't want to live here. I have a whole life back home. A business. Animals to take care of." Her eyes flicked to mine, and her expression hardened. "A boyfriend. I can't just up and leave."

The thought of her having some pencil-dicked boyfriend waiting for her back in Alaska had me white-knuckling the arms of my chair. It shouldn't, but it did.

"Tell him you'll be gone longer than you thought, sparrow. This house has been in my family for a hundred years. I won't lose it because you can't keep a bargain."

"Is it a bargain if it's forced on me? A gilded cage is still a cage."

"Oh yeah, you're really the inconvenienced party here. Cry me a fucking river, *River*."

"Cute."

"You used to think so."

"Used to is the operative phrase there." She cut a glance at McCreedy. "Are we done here? I have a hotel room waiting for me in town."

McCreedy cleared his throat, but years of working for my family kept his expression blank. "It behooves me to inform you, Miss Adams, that the clock starts after you spend your first night under this roof. Although there is a clause that allows you seven days to begin your tenure here, I would suggest you make alternative arrangements so you may begin your stay tonight. After seven days, however, your shares will be null and void as outlined in the document."

"The sooner we get this year over with, the sooner you can get out of my hair and sell me back my life," I grumbled. "I'm not giving up everything because you're a stubborn, spoiled brat. Call your hotel. Cancel your registration. Don't worry about your clothes, you can buy more. God knows you have enough money now. The countdown begins tonight."

three
...
River

I might as well have been staying in a hotel for all the personality the guest room offered here at the ranch. Walker had offered me the primary suite, saying it was technically mine now, but the thought of sleeping in Senior's old room creeped me out. Instead, I'd claimed the room I'd always used whenever I spent the night here. While I'm sure a few things had changed over the years, to my eye it was exactly the same. Same bed, same desk, same pictures on the wall. It even smelled the same.

The only thing different was the attached bathroom. Senior had upgraded it to include not only a large walk-in shower, but an epic egg-shaped soaking tub. I saw myself spending hours in that thing. I had close to ten thousand hours to spare until I could get out of here. I was pretty sure I could waste at least half of those taking long, luxurious bubble baths. That would probably piss Cross off, especially if I used all the hot water every day.

The likelihood of that in a place this size was pretty much nonexistent, but I had my Petty Betty pants firmly in place and no intention of removing them anytime soon.

Restless energy coursed through me at the thought of

having to stay here, with *him*, for so much longer than I'd planned. But now that Senior'd had his say, I had no other options. Especially not with the ticking bomb in my luggage. I was trapped here for the sake of so much more than a house and some property.

My hands shook as I unzipped my overnight bag, pulling out the manila envelope I'd stashed inside for safekeeping. I'd always thought a package like this would come with serial killer handwriting or letters cut out from a glossy magazine. But even without those classic details, it felt sinister enough to be a threat. My name was the only thing scrawled across the front, which meant someone had been tracking me. That was the only way for it to show up at my little Alaskan hideaway like it did, shoved into the mail slot and waiting for me to wake up.

That thought alone was terrifying. What had I done to earn myself a stalker?

But it was so much worse than that because whoever my mysterious pen pal was, they weren't interested in me. Not really. This was about my parents. More specifically, the manner of their death.

Just reaching for the contents made my heart race, even though I already knew what was inside. The images burned themselves into my brain after my initial inspection, and I'd never be able to unsee them.

Nausea was a ball in my stomach as I pulled out the stack of crime scene photos, the little Post-it fluttering down to my lap as my eyes zeroed in on the destruction captured in all its horrific glory. I knew the mangled car well, but now it looked like nothing more than a lump made of sharp edges and broken glass. It was impossible to look away from the sight because my mother's sightless eyes stared at nothing from where her body had been laid out right next to my father.

Bright red blood covered their clothes. Mom's favorite date night dress and Dad's white button-down a shocking crimson. They'd told me the accident had killed them instantly, but this said differently. These photos were clear as day. And so were the bullet holes in each of my parents' foreheads.

I picked up the sticky note and swallowed the bile threatening to rise in my throat.

> ***It wasn't an accident.***
> ***They're not who you think they are.***

This was the real reason I'd be staying in Devil's Grove, Texas, for the foreseeable future. Not because of the Cross family. Not because of some ridiculous will. My parents were murdered.

And I was here to figure out who killed them.

I'D MISSED a lot of things about Texas when I moved away ten years ago, but the oppressive heat wasn't one of them. As I walked the grounds, headed for the stables, I wiped sweat off my brow and wished like hell I'd brought something more appropriate for the warm weather. I swore I could feel myself getting sunburnt through my jeans. At least I'd thought to bring a tank top.

Something in my chest loosened as the barn came into view, only to immediately seize up again as I noticed the man sitting in the shade polishing tack. The enormous man. His face was obscured by the brim of his straw cowboy hat, but I didn't need to see his features to know he was formidable.

"Who the fuck are you?" he grunted without looking up at me.

I stopped, one hand on my hip as I assessed him. "Who the fuck are *you*?"

"You're not supposed to be here. Cross told Walker not to let his buckle bunnies roam the grounds unattended. This is a working ranch. It's not some resort."

Anger swelled hot and fast. I blamed my run-in with Cross for a lot of that. I was usually a pretty even-keeled girl and knew how to keep a level head no matter the situation. After the last ten years, I'd needed to. I wouldn't have survived otherwise. But being back here with hundreds of memories haunting me, I had none of my usual cool.

"Who the hell are you calling a buckle bunny, you sorry excuse for a rodeo clown?"

Bear would be proud of me. He'd taught me to fight for my place in the world. Stand my ground and not let anyone walk all over me just because I looked sweet.

That got the surly cowboy to look up from what he was doing, his bearded jaw not hiding the twitch of his lips. "I call 'em like I see 'em. I know a bunny when I see one."

"Is that how you talk to your boss?"

Gunmetal gray irises, a color I'd never seen, locked on mine. "What?"

Bolstering myself with all the bravado I could muster, I approached him, hand outstretched. "River Adams. New owner of Twisted Cross Ranch. And you are?"

"Bishop."

Apparently that was all he intended to say on the matter. He also didn't offer me his hand.

"Is that your only name? Traditionally most people have two."

"It's the only one I'm going to give you until I verify your story. I don't make a habit of giving strangers personal details about myself."

"You don't make a habit of manners, either."

He grunted.

"So the southern gentleman gene skipped you, huh? Noted."

"Suppose so."

"How many of you are there?"

Bishop went back to polishing the tack he still held between his fingers. "Well, boss, I guess that's something you should do your research on, now isn't it?"

The temptation to pop him right in his pretty face was high. Sadly, it wasn't the urge to turn to violence that shocked me.

Pretty? We think the asshole is pretty? What the hell is wrong with you, River, that you step one foot back on this ranch and are immediately attracted to toxic men?

"It seems like it. Maybe I'll look into budget cuts while I'm at it. My asshole quota has already been filled."

His lips twitched, and what could have been a snort of amusement or derision left him as he stood. He sauntered past me without so much as a 'how do,' leaving me to gape after his towering form. The guy was six-five, six-six—maybe taller—and built with the kind of muscles only years of hands-on hard work could create. He was all coiled power and grace, wrapped up in ironclad control. This was not a man prone to fits of whimsy. Just one interaction had been enough to show me that. He was all about structure, and anyone who threatened that stability was to be held in the highest suspicion, if not outright mistrust.

Put all of those things together, and I had no trouble imagining him in fatigues. Or a loincloth . . . all oiled up, maybe?

Jesus, River.

What could I say? I'd been going through a dry spell, and coming back here was like offering salt water to someone stranded in the desert. It would be really bad for me, but that didn't mean I wouldn't crave it. Cowboys were my weakness. They always had been.

I swallowed, my throat suddenly parched as he faded

from view, but the deep rumble of his voice still echoed in my mind. Why was I attracted to mean men? First Cross, now Bishop.

No.

Cross was off the table. Just because he was handsome and perfect and he made me feel like the only girl in the world one time didn't give him a place in my heart. No matter how many flutters he set off in my bathing suit parts.

Though I'd be lying if I said anyone else came close to matching those flutters.

I'd had other partners in the last ten years, obviously. But no one held a candle to Cross and the things he'd done to my body. In a matter of hours, he'd ruined me for anyone else. And I was still paying for it years later.

Bastard.

My phone buzzed from my back pocket, startling me out of my Cross-induced spiral. God, I didn't want to be here. I was already losing sight of who I'd worked so hard to become simply because the man was in my vicinity.

Pulling my cell free, I glanced at the screen, grinning as the only name I expected to see was displayed. Bear. My protector. My confidant.

BEAR: You were supposed to text me when you landed. It's been hours.

Me: Sorry. It's been crazy. And we both know you tracked my flight the whole way here, so you already know I landed safely.

Bear: So? We had a deal. You go without me, you check in regularly.

Bear: How you holding up, cub?

Me: It's about what I expected. Give or take a few surprises.

. . .

WELL, that was certainly one way to frame how Senior had pulled the rug out from beneath us all.

BEAR: **Need me to come down there?**

THE OFFER WAS A TEMPTING ONE. More for the support than the protection. But there's no way the Cross brothers would react well to a man like Bear showing up on their property. My property?

I sighed, already picturing how that would play out. Best to leave it as my 'nuclear' option.

ME: **No.**
   Me: Not yet.

four

Walker

Thirteen years earlier

$\mathcal{S}$he's so fucking pretty.

I couldn't contain the thought as I watched my best friend. River was a blur as she raced across the pasture, hair flying behind her, laugh taunting me from where I sat atop Blue.

"Catch me if you can!" she called before leaning forward and pushing Kismet harder. The horse sped up, and that was all the encouragement I needed.

I dug my heels into Blue's side and clicked my tongue. My pretty mare might have seemed soft and gentle, but she was damn fast. It wasn't long before we were right on their heels, Blue's strides eating up the ground between us until we were neck and neck.

"To the tree?" I asked, breathless from the rush.

River's eyes sparkled as she nodded, then gave Kismet another nudge.

The two of us ended up reaching our tree at the same time, but I let her think she won. It was worth it to see the smile light up her face as she dismounted and tied Kismet to the hitching post nearby.

"That was a close one."

I'd always been competitive—some might even call me a poor sport—but with River looking the way she did, things had changed. Now I didn't care one bit about losing or my pride. Something had shifted between us, and I had a pretty good idea of what it was. The difference between fifteen and sixteen was a big one for me. Especially where River was concerned.

It's like I woke up one morning and the girl who'd been my best friend for the last ten years was a stranger. Suddenly I was noticing things like the way her eyes crinkled when she smiled, the number of freckles she had across the bridge of her nose, how good she smelled, or more recently, the way her denim was just a bit tighter in the hips and it made my mouth go dry.

So . . . not best friend thoughts.

The problem was, River definitely wasn't on the same page. She looked at me and still saw her buddy Walker. I didn't know how to change that without ruining what we had. What if I made a move and she rejected me? Could I recover from that? Could our friendship survive?

A big part of me held on to the conversation I'd had with Cross not long ago. He was so much older, with a lot more experience with girls. He knew about this stuff.

"You have to take your shot, or you'll waste your chance. Don't sit there with your thumb up your ass. Ladies like confidence. Take what you want. Don't make her guess, because nine times outta ten, she's going to assume you're not interested and set her sights on someone else."

River and I sat under the shade of the big old oak, the

silence between us as comfortable as it always was. She leaned her head on my shoulder and sighed, and it was all I could do not to inhale the scent of her hair.

If I just dipped my chin down, my lips would brush her forehead. Or, even better, I could tip her chin up, and then I could just kiss her.

My heart raced, and my palms grew sweaty at the thought.

I couldn't think of anything else. I wanted to know if she'd taste like that pineapple chapstick she always wore.

"River," I murmured, desperate to catch her attention so I could do what Cross had said and take what I wanted. Make my move.

"Yeah?" Here it was, the chance I needed. She shifted and began turning her head toward mine but stopped, her focus snapping to the rider galloping across the pasture in the distance.

My brother.

The look on her face said it all. Especially when he stopped and lifted his shirt to wipe the sweat from his brow. She wanted him.

Not me.

Never me.

I would always be runner-up. The spare, never the heir. Just like everyone loved to remind me.

I was honestly surprised I even had a name. Dad should have just called me Two. That would have been clearer.

"Walker, are you even listening to me?"

Present day

"WALKER, are you even listening to me?"

My brother's words echoed the same ones River had used so long ago, snapping me out of the memory.

I scowled down at the woman in question as I watched her from the window, phone in her hand, her lips curled up in that same doting expression she used to reserve for Cross.

Must be talking to the boyfriend.

"Walker! Get your head out of your ass."

"What?" I snapped.

"You might not be worried about her coming in and taking over, but I sure as fuck am. I don't know what Dad thought he was doing."

"I dunno, seems like classic Senior to me."

"This isn't a game. She can't run this ranch, not to mention everything else we have going on. She shouldn't be here."

Maybe not, but it wasn't like she was going anywhere anytime soon. Not unless we wanted to lose everything we'd spent our lives building.

"Well, news flash, brother. She's here. There ain't nothing we can do about it."

Cross dragged a hand through his hair and growled. "That old asshole. Dictating our lives even after he died."

"Like I said, classic Senior. Are you really surprised? The man lived to boss us and everyone else around. Pretty sure he thought he was some kind of king."

"More like kingpin," Cross muttered.

That was true enough, given that the bulk of his empire was of the illegal variety.

"I'll keep her distracted from the less-than-savory stuff. You keep everything else going, all right? You've made it clear you don't want her here, so there's no use in trying to put the two of you together."

Cross nodded curtly, his gaze refusing to go to the window. "Keep her out of my way. She might own the legit businesses, but I run this ship. I'll just have to do it under the radar." He checked his phone as he spoke, brows pulling down and a scowl making him look meaner than a hornet. "Speaking of. I need to go."

"What's up?"

"Nothing you need to worry about. Watch her. Don't let her get too curious."

I raised a brow. "We talking about the same girl? You do remember River, right? Surest way to pique her interest is to try and distract her." The girl had been a regular Nancy Drew when we were kids. Always snooping around, trying to suss out everyone's secrets. Not that she called it that. She referred to it as investigating. But it was the same thing.

"Well, figure it out, because unless you want to explain just what it is we're shipping in our trucks, that's precisely what you need to do."

My gut churned. The last thing she needed to know was the finer details of Cross Transport and Freight's cargo. Beef and cattle weren't the only things we shipped across the country. Something told me she wasn't the drug-running type. Or weapons, for that matter.

Not that the drugs were the fun kind. We were talking pharmaceuticals, but I didn't think she'd appreciate the distinction with our clients being who they were. Neither would the DEA. Unfortunately, this wasn't a life you could just *leave*.

Blood in, blood out. Wasn't that the saying? And fuck if it wasn't true. This was the only life we'd ever known, and even if our dad was a dick, he protected what was his. Cross and I would do the same. This ranch and the people loyal to us mattered.

So I'd do what I did best. I'd distract the fuck out of River Adams.

My eyes wandered back out the window to the woman

outside. She was even more beautiful than she'd been the last time I saw her. I'd distract her, all right.

And maybe this time, I'd get to keep the girl.

After all, River isn't the only one all grown up.

five

River

I gave myself exactly one evening to sulk. I took full advantage of the wine cellar and that fancy new tub they'd installed in my room. Cried. Ranted. Cried some more. But they were angry tears. You know the ones, where you're so frustrated by your situation that you just need to purge some of the overwhelming emotion so you can think straight and then focus on taking down your enemy? Yeah, that kind.

Thank God this house was so damn huge. Unless they were spying on me, the Cross brothers wouldn't have heard me sobbing in the tub. I made a mental note to check for cameras and listening devices because I wouldn't put it past Daniel Cross Jr. to do exactly that. He trusted me about as far as he could throw me.

I didn't even trust him as far as *I* could throw *him*. So there.

This morning had been the silent treatment as we both got our coffee—we being Cross and I, Walker never rose before noon if he didn't have to—then a little people watching from the kitchen window as I drank said coffee. The view was nice, especially the cowboys working in the distance and that ranch hand, Bishop, as he mended a bit of fence nearby. That man had a lot going for him. One, he was fuck hot. Two, he wasn't related to the Cross family. Three, he screamed 'mysterious past,' and that really appealed to the part of me that loved uncovering secrets.

In another life, I think I might have liked being a private investigator. I loved my true crime podcasts and always tried to solve the crimes while listening. Spoiler alert, it's almost always the husband. 'Never meet a man,' as one of my favorite podcasters always says.

Preach, sister. Words to live by for sure. Men are trouble.

Exhibit giant D stalked into the kitchen, poured himself a fresh cup of coffee, tossed me a mean-as-hell glare, and stormed back out. Whatever. I had my very own cowboy revue outside. I didn't need him.

My phone chirped with a text notification, pulling my gaze from the landscape of hot guys and horses.

GIGI:

> Got your email this morning. Thanks for taking care of that. I don't know why there were duplicate journal entries. Accounting is so not my thing.

ME:

> That's why you have me. It absolutely is mine.

GIGI:

> Thank God for that. Anyone who enjoys math should be canonized for sainthood. Or detained in a ring of salt until they can be tested for demonic energy.

ME:

> You've been reading those paranormal romances again, haven't you?

> **GIGI:**
> He has a TAIL, and he knows how to use it.
> 😈

> **ME:**
> Well, when you put it that way . . . Send me the link.

A book link came through point two seconds later, followed by another text.

> **GIGI:**
> So, how's the cowboy life? Bear said you're stuck there.

> **ME:**
> The view is nice. The company is . . . icy.

> **GIGI:**
> Icy can be fun. We love a reason to bundle or cozy up in front of the fireplace.

I rolled my eyes. Despite her rather disastrous love life, Gigi was a hopeless romantic and unapologetic about it. I loved that about her, but she saw love where it wasn't more often than not. The last blind date she sent me on ended in misery because of her terrible matchmaking skills.

> **ME:**
> Not when he's so cold he gives me frostbite.

> **GIGI:**
> Yeah, that's less hot. No one needs frosty flaps.

I snorted and shook my head, her texts making me more homesick by the second.

ME:

> Anyway, enough about he who shall not be acknowledged. Senior left me a whole house and a lot of his businesses. I need to work on getting things in order.

GIGI:

> If anyone can make those books her bitch, it's you! You'll be done before you know it and back here where you belong.

I didn't have the heart, or stomach really, to mention the one-year shackle holding me hostage. Seemed like a conversation best had over wine. Or maybe a bottle of tequila.

ME:

> Miss you, G.

GIGI:

> I know. Talk soon.

After draining my mug, I placed it in the sink and brushed my hands together, the universal sign for *let's get this show on the road*.

The house was . . . fucking huge. At least five thousand square feet and a sprawling U shape. One thing about the Cross family was they liked to ensure everyone had their own space. Even the ranch foreman had his own room in the house if he wanted it. The interior design said rustic but richer than God. Antler chandeliers, stonework fireplaces that rarely got used because this was Texas and it was hot as balls, and high-end artisan furniture I was pretty sure no one ever sat on. My dad once told me the leather for the couches was sourced from Twisted Cross Ranch's own cows.

I shook my head, overwhelmed by the excess that surrounded me. Excess that was technically now mine. I wondered if I looked as out of place as I felt. Because while I grew up in this world, it was nothing like my life back in

Alaska. I'd had to fight tooth and nail for everything I had. I'd earned my sweet little house with literal blood, sweat, and tears. Bear had helped me at first, but over time I'd learned how to do the repairs myself. I spent weekends combing through antique shops, building bookshelves, or upcycling my new coffee table until I finally had my sanctuary exactly how I wanted it.

In fact, my house could probably fit inside the Cross's formal living room. Of course there was more than one. There were actually three, if we were getting precious about it.

A couple of cowboys stood around the island in the kitchen at the far end of the house, helpfully labeled *Cowboy Kitchen*. I gave them a little wave and continued on my exploration mission. I needed to get reacquainted with this home if I was going to get any information. That note I'd received directed me here, encouraging me to stay and solve the mystery of my parents' deaths. So I would go through every book, every drawer and closet, and search for any scrap of evidence I could find that might lead me to answers.

THREE HOURS, two additional cups of coffee, and countless dead ends later, I finally stumbled across something that seemed promising. I sequestered myself in Senior's office, though I supposed it was my office now. With rich hunter-green walls, dark mahogany bookcases, and a cowskin rug on the floor, I could practically smell the spice of Senior's cologne in here. It was almost like any minute he'd walk in the room and catch me going through his stuff.

Maybe it felt that way because *I* felt like I was snooping. It didn't matter how many times I told myself I had every right to look through the reports and files regarding my new businesses, or that this was no different than what I did for the companies I worked for back home. It still felt shady. Probably because I had an ulterior motive.

Logically, I knew I wasn't going to open up a desk drawer and find a literal smoking gun. But I knew enough from working with Bear, whose colorful past taught me that companies have as much to hide as individuals. And that no one was squeaky clean. So there should be something in here to lead me in the right direction. Otherwise, what was the point of sending me those pictures?

Without access to the password that would unlock the laptop and the multitude of data it contained, I was limited to hard copies only. Unfortunately, rifling through the desk drawers only gave me access to generic, uninteresting things like business cards, pens, and other office supplies. I did find a bottle of top-shelf whiskey in the bottom drawer, three-quarters full even.

"Thank you, Senior. Don't mind if I do." I tipped the bottle back and took a sip, shuddering at the burn of the alcohol.

When I went to put it back, my fingers brushed against something that felt like a notch in the wood. It was small, barely noticeable. I probably would have never caught it if my fingertips hadn't run against the little divot.

"What is that?" I murmured, pressing down and gasping at the soft click as a false drawer opened up and revealed a maroon leather portfolio. "Senior, you shady bastard. What are you hiding?"

Until this moment, I hadn't actually entertained the idea that Senior had been personally involved in my parent's death. But now, knowing he was hiding things in his own home, it seemed a lot more plausible.

How well did I really know Daniel Cross Senior?

Not at all, apparently.

Placing the folder on the desktop, I took a few deep breaths to steady myself before I opened it. Part of me didn't want to know if the Crosses had anything to do with my parents dying, but another begged for this to be the end of my search. I flipped the folio open with shaking hands, bracing myself for the worst. Instead I stared down at a handwritten ledger filled with expenses and income, names, and dates. A few entries were even written in some kind of code.

I sat back in the executive chair with an audible gasp. I knew what this was. I'd scrimped and saved to put myself through school so I could become an accountant. I'd also helped Bear manage more than one shady set of accounts for a hefty fee. My burly protector might be a teddy bear to me, but the club he was part of was hardly made up of a bunch of boy scouts. He took me in and taught me how to fend for myself, but some of those lessons weren't exactly legal, if you catch my drift. He thought it was important that a girl on her own learn how to recognize red flags in all their forms. His first lesson: you couldn't protect yourself if you didn't realize you were being had. That wasn't just true in business, but life in general. Which is how I scored my first bookkeeping job. The Timberline MC thought one of their affiliates was stealing from them. He asked me to follow the money and sniff the rat out.

When they realized I had a knack for numbers, they kept me on. TMC had more than its share of income streams, and someone had to keep it all clean for them. Tax evasion was one thing. Laundering was something else.

Which brought me back to what I was looking at now. This was *definitely* something else.

Senior had a second set of books. Twisted Cross Ranch had dipped its fingers into something dark, and I needed to know everything.

I snagged my phone and dialed Jackson McCreedy's number as I flipped through page after page of Senior's dealings. This journal was years old. Filled to nearly the last page.

"McCreedy here," Jackson answered on the second ring.

"Mr. McCreedy, this is River Adams. I need your help with something."

"Well, it'd be my pleasure, Ms. Adams. What can I do for you?" Something in his voice clued me in to the fact that it was about as far from a pleasurable task as he could imagine.

I pushed back the nerves racing through my stomach and pressed on. "I'm going to need every password, every key to the locks on this ranch, and access to all of Senior's accounts. Cross might think he can keep me in the dark about Cross Industries, but I'm not the kind of woman who buries her head in the sand."

He spluttered for a moment, then sighed. "Very well. I'll do what I can. It might take me a few—"

"I expect them to be delivered to me by the end of the day today."

Without giving him a chance to respond, I hung up and went back to inspecting Senior's books, making notes about things to follow up on or dig into further. With each new line item I added, the ball of dread in my belly grew heavier. This was incriminating evidence, something that could land the whole family in jail. I was part owner now, and that meant my own freedom was at risk.

My blood turned to ice when I caught sight of one large transaction the day after my eighteenth birthday. The same day I left.

Casey Adams – $500,000 Security

Why was Senior paying half a million dollars to my dad? What kind of security did he need? Thinking back on it now, had my father agreed to let me go stay with my grandmother too easily? Had it even been my idea? That day was such a blur of heartbreak; I'd been so focused on the note Cross had left for me, the way he'd destroyed me without so much as a backward glance. I never stopped to consider anything other than getting as far away from him as possible.

"Fuck. Fuck fuck fuck," I whispered, slamming the ledger closed and turning the chair around to stare out the window. "Is this what got you dead, Daddy? Did you find out something you weren't supposed to know? Get into bed with a snake?" I was hardly the same naïve eighteen-year-old girl I'd been, but I just couldn't imagine my dad willingly participating in something that would put my mama and me in harm's way.

Then again, they say you never really knew a person. Had he been a stranger all along?

six

Cross

My feet slapped hard on the treadmill as I sprinted at top speed during my final high-intensity interval. I wasn't afforded the luxury of time outside like the rest of the guys who worked on this ranch. Now that my dad was gone, it was meetings, phone calls, and more meetings—and none of them were relaxed or fucking fun. And that was just the up and up side of the family business.

The other, seedier side was more hands-on, but took place under cover of darkness. Those meetings had the potential to get more physical, but Walker handled them more often than not. I only got involved when a message needed to be sent. I had to keep my hands clean until it was absolutely necessary to get them dirty.

The music blaring in my ears cut off as a phone call came through my earbuds. Speaking of my relentless schedule . . .

Hitting the quick stop on the machine, I got off and answered, barking a curt, "Cross," as I worked to catch my breath.

"Fucking or fighting?" McCreedy asked, half-serious.

"Neither."

He made a soft non-committal sound that could have been

a laugh. Bastard knew if he tried that shit in front of me, he'd be eating my fist.

"What do you want?" I snapped, a headache already building at the base of my skull.

"Your little heiress has started digging already. She's asking for keys and passwords."

My teeth clenched hard enough that the headache burst to vibrant life behind my eye. "So give her the ones she can have."

"Did you know she's a corporate accountant? I've been looking into her background since she got here. She's dangerous."

"You don't fucking say."

I hadn't known she was a number-cruncher. How would I? We weren't exactly bosom buddies. But that girl had had danger written all over her from day one. Well, from the day I noticed her anyway.

"Something tells me she's not going to stop at passwords, Cross. She'll keep digging. And one day, she'll find something."

If she hadn't already.

"I'll handle it."

"Better you than me. If I have to get involved . . ."

I didn't need him to finish that sentence. Once McCreedy was involved, things best left in the dark would come to light. I couldn't let that happen. He might've helped keep our dirty little secrets hidden, but River was too close to this. She was smart, and she'd figure him—and, by association, us—out.

Just the thought alone was enough to send my pulse skyrocketing. Everything would be ruined. We'd lose, and this couldn't all have been for nothing. The shit I'd done. The blood on my hands. The things we'd covered up. She'd never see us as anything other than villains if she found out. But what was worse, if she learned the truth, that would mean I gave her up for no fucking reason.

"Dammit, sparrow, why couldn't you just stay gone," I grumbled as I snagged a towel and wiped the sweat from my neck.

I needed a goddamned shower before I did anything else, but the knot of apprehension in my gut wouldn't let me divert my attention away from the problem at hand. River.

Normally I liked to appear put together, confident and collected. Cold. The best way to make people fear you was to look untouchable. Like there wasn't a weakness they could exploit because you knew and accepted all facets of yourself beyond the shadow of a doubt. I couldn't do that sweaty and in gym shorts.

"Cross?" McCreedy said, reminding me he was still on the phone.

"I said I'll handle her."

"She wants everything by the end of the day. I can't put her off long."

"I'm on it." I hung up and shoved my phone in my pocket, frustration coiling the muscles in my shoulders as I left the gym and made my way to the central foyer connecting all three wings of the U-shaped lodge.

"River Adams, get your pretty ass down here!"

As soon as I opened my mouth and hollered her name, I knew it was the wrong approach, but I was too pissed off to care. I also hadn't really expected an answer, but it only made my temper swell. I was not a man used to being ignored.

I prowled down the hallway leading to my father's office. Given the demands she'd made of McCreedy, it was the most logical place she could be.

"Sparrow!" I was not a fan of the silent treatment, especially not from her.

Sure, I'd earned it, but . . .

"Jesus Christ, what? Is the lodge on fire? Why are you screaming for me?" She skidded out of the office and met me in the hall, nearly crashing into my bare chest.

For a second, I'd forgotten why I was so angry. All I could focus on was how she perfectly lined up with me. She'd always been tall, but she'd filled out in the years since I'd last seen her up close and biblically. Now was not the time to remember what her tight little cunt felt like, but my mind went there anyway. I was damn near mute as I recalled with precise clarity the way it felt to be sheathed inside her while she milked my cock for every last drop.

"Well? Are you going to stand there sweating all over me, or is there a reason you hollered loud enough to shake the windows?" She crossed her arms over her chest, only adding to the ache in my balls.

Fuck, I was wearing gym shorts, and if I didn't stop thinking about all the ways I'd touched her that night, there'd be no hiding what she did to me. As it was, I was already breathing like an enraged bull.

Fuck or fight, isn't that what McCreedy asked? Since option one was off the table, I guess we were stuck with door number two.

"You'll get your damn passwords and keys when I'm good and ready," I growled.

She blew out a breath, grumbling something that sounded like "I should have known he'd run and tattle. Same little weasel he's always been." But when she looked back at me, she was every inch the collected businessperson that I pretended to be. "Not your call to make."

"You might have the shares, sparrow, but it's my name on the letterhead. What I say goes. Ask anyone here and they'll tell you the same."

She stepped closer to me, her eyes flashing with challenge. "Legally, I could toss you out on your ass right now. You're only here because I'm not a complete bitch. Test me and see how long that lasts."

"Legally, you can't. It was one of the terms, remember? Or

do you need me to point to the fine print, your royal highness? We stay. End of story."

"Not if I let everything go to the trust. I could leave right now, and you lose it all. Face it, Cross. You. Need. Me." She poked my chest on the last word, and I instinctively caught her by the wrist.

"Don't push me. I might not look it, but I've got a mean streak a mile long."

Her eyes narrowed. "So do I."

I couldn't help it. I laughed. Sparrow looked about as mean as her namesake. She was all long legs, supple curves, and flushed cheeks. A guy like me could chew her up and spit her out without breaking a sweat. The girl who gave me her virginity and told me she loved me was too sweet for this life.

Time to call her bluff.

"Do you? You sure didn't look mean when you stared into my eyes and said you loved me."

"Biggest mistake I ever made." She jerked out of my hold and stepped back. "It should have been Walker."

I saw red. Before I made the conscious decision to do it, my hand was wrapped around her throat, and I shoved her up against the wall, my body crowding hers.

"You wanna say that again, sparrow?"

Dragging in a shuddering breath, she glanced down at my mouth briefly before dragging her gaze to my eyes.

"Do I need to spell it out for you?"

"I think so." My hips pressed against hers, the obvious erection I couldn't hide grinding into her belly. "Draw it out, nice and slow. Tell me exactly how much you hate me for what I did to you. Tell me how you didn't beg me to fuck you. How you didn't cry out my name and scratch up my back while you clung to me, coming so hard you nearly blacked out. Tell me it was all a lie."

"You're the liar. Not me."

I leaned close, running my nose along the side of her face,

letting my lips drag across her cheek. "I never lied. You just couldn't see the truth."

"Cross . . ."

"You still want me, sparrow? Do you touch yourself at night and remember what you let me do?"

Instead of giving me what I wanted, she swallowed, her pulse fluttering beneath my hold. "Do you?"

"Every. Fucking. Night," I growled, stealing her lips and branding her with my kiss.

She melted against me for one beautiful moment before pain blossomed across my lower lip as her teeth sank into my flesh.

"Fuck!" I cursed, pulling back and wiping my hand across my now bleeding lip.

"Touch me again and I'll make sure you don't have anything to stroke at night."

My lips curled up in a wicked grin. She might be threatening me with her words, but she was fucking me with her eyes. "Might be fun to see you try. But you get your hands anywhere near my cock, sparrow, and we're gonna be playing a whole different game. You're not a virgin anymore. I don't have to be sweet or gentle."

"Get me the damn keys, Cross. I'm done playing anything with you."

I backed away, releasing her throat and adjusting myself just as Bishop's tall frame appeared at the end of the hallway.

"Everything okay out here, boss?" he asked, brow furrowed, gaze locked on the woman I'd pinned to the wall.

"Fine. I was just reminding Junior here who his new boss is." She patted me on the shoulder. "You really need to shower. You're a mess, and you should do something about your chapped lips. They're bleeding."

She pushed past me without another look. Bishop waited until she reached him, tossing me one last unreadable look before heading off after her.

I blew out a breath, realizing that while I'd been the one to call her bluff, she walked away with the upper hand. I came out of this encounter looking like the asshole I wanted her to see me as, but I also wanted her even more now that she'd shown me that spark. This was a lose-lose situation.

"Sonofabitch!" Fist clenched, I punched the wall so hard the drywall caved in and pain radiated through my knuckles.

And now I had another mess to deal with.

Fucking perfect.

seven

. . .

Bishop

"You don't have to follow me," River said as she stormed outside into the bright afternoon sun.

"Yeah, I do."

When she got to the shade of a big old oak, she whirled around to face me. "Why? Did he put you up to this? Are you supposed to watch me and make sure I don't step out of line?"

I almost laughed because it couldn't be further from the truth. Right on the heels of that impulse came shock, because I couldn't remember the last time I'd found anything remotely funny.

My world was a dark place filled with the ghosts of my past. I kept myself busy so I wouldn't have to listen to the screams. So I could try, as long as possible, to forget. These days, duty was the only thing keeping me sane.

"No."

"You're a real chatterbox, aren't you?"

"No."

Her eyes crinkled at the corners as her lips quirked into a smile.

It was then I saw the blood on her lip, and a cold pit

formed in my stomach. Anger barrelled through me as I reached out to wipe away the blood without conscious thought. The heat of her burned, and I froze for a second as I realized that for the first time since returning to the States, I'd willingly touched another person. Isolation had been the only coping mechanism I had.

Darkness threatened in the periphery, the agonized wails filling my ears. I forced myself to breathe, to focus on the present and remind myself that I was safe.

When I spoke again, my voice was little more than a gravel-filled rasp. "He hurt you."

Eyes wide, she shook her head. "It's not mine. I bit him."

Relief hit me square in the chest. I really hadn't wanted to kill Cross, but with the way I'd reacted to the idea of him hurting her, that's where this was headed. I shouldn't be so focused on her. I didn't know the woman. I didn't owe her shit.

And yet . . .

I'd felt it the second those emerald eyes pierced mine. A sense of longing for the one thing I didn't have. A place I could lie down and rest. Home.

She lured me in as surely as a siren did a ship at sea.

It made her dangerous in a way a man like Cross could never be.

I needed to be careful around her. I'd forget why I was here. Forget my job and my responsibilities, and fall into her deep green eyes.

"Bishop?" she ventured, making me realize I was standing there staring at her.

What had we been talking about? Oh, right. It was *his* blood.

"Good."

Her brows rose, and her lips twitched again. "Good? I just bit your boss, and you think that's good?"

In my line of work, violence was not only expected, it was encouraged. I shrugged. "He probably had it coming."

She surprised me by humming a few bars of an old musical number before agreeing, "That he did."

"History?" I asked, sensing that there was a lot more to that story.

"You could say that."

I waited to see if she'd elaborate, but instead she walked along the fenceline, and I followed. There was just something about her that made me want to stay in her orbit.

"I can take care of myself, you know?" she tossed over her shoulder.

"I'm just walking with you."

"And watching me like a hawk."

"Maybe you need watching."

She spun around, hands on her hips. "I'd find that offensive if I wasn't so sure you believed it." Her eyes narrowed as she studied me. It was hard not to fidget under her inspection. She saw too much. I knew it the second her expression softened and her hands fell. "You're ex-military, aren't you?"

My gut churned. I didn't talk about my time as a SEAL for lots of reasons. One, I'd seen some shit. Shit I couldn't come back from. There was no fucking way I'd darken her mind with my nightmares.

"How'd you know?"

"It's the haunted look in your eyes. A friend of mine was special ops. He took me under his wing too. He said he was never the same, but it helped to have a purpose. Something to focus on besides his memories."

Was that what I was doing? Taking her under my wing?

"Distractions are important."

"Do you have nightmares?"

She reached for me, and I flinched away from her touch on instinct. "Please don't . . . I don't like to be touched."

Jesus, this woman was disarming. Usually I didn't even let myself get close enough for it to be an issue.

Understanding flitted across her face, and she pulled her hand back. "My apologies."

"No, I'm sorry . . ."

"You have no reason to apologize. I shouldn't have assumed. You're entitled to your boundaries, Bishop. Same as everybody else."

Swallowing hard, I pulled my shit together and nodded. "If he touches you again without your consent, tell me. I don't care who he is. I'll put a stop to it."

"Why are you so invested in me? You don't know me."

I shrugged and kept walking, my eyes on the horizon as we approached the small pond near the stables. There were a lot of answers I could give her, all of which were true, but I settled on the simplest.

"He's not a good man, River."

She stiffened. "I know."

"You deserve a good man."

Her brows flew up again as we reached the old oak and the wooden swing hanging from one of its boughs. Settling herself onto the bench, she looked up at me. "Are you an expert on what I need already, Bishop?"

"One look at you and I can tell you're pure. I've known men like him before. He'll tarnish you so quick you won't recognize yourself."

Her eyes went wide for a second before she snorted. "My, the image you have of me. It's going to hurt when I fall off that pedestal. And I will fall, Bishop. I'm not the wholesome little girl you think I am."

Some of the darkness I recognized filtered through her eyes, and it gutted me. No one should have to carry that kind of burden. It's the reason men like me enlisted in the first place. We were supposed to protect and shelter the people back home. But no one had been there to shelter River, and now she was in the thick of it. Thrust straight into a pit of vipers.

Good thing she had me.

Wait. What?

Where the hell had that come from?

Fuck, I was in trouble.

Using her toes, she swayed on the swing, back and forth, as she gazed out over the land.

"You know, I used to love it here. When I was a kid, this was my favorite place."

"And now?"

"Now it feels more like a prison."

I, better than most, knew what that was like. I wanted to reach out and give her a push, help her fly and feel her warmth against my rough palm. But I stopped myself as soon as that familiar anxiety gripped my chest.

"Why stay then?"

"I don't have a choice."

"There's always a choice."

She shook her head. "No. Sometimes there's only one path, even if people try to make you think otherwise."

I remained rooted to the spot, processing her words. She seemed so resigned to her fate. "Are they keeping you here? It doesn't look like you're loyal to Cross."

"No. But remember all those people who rely on this place to feed their families? I'm responsible for them now. If I leave, this place is gone. Their jobs aren't protected anymore."

"What do you mean by that?"

She huffed out a bitter laugh. "How long do you have before you have to get back to work?"

Walking around so I could lean against the tree and look at her, I leveled my gaze on her beautiful face. "You're the boss, you tell me. Because if you need me to listen, I've got all damn day."

After a few silent beats, she sighed and began, "It's complicated..."

The longer she went on, outlining the terms of her inheritance, the more I realized that *complicated* was an understatement. They had her so wrapped up in legal barbed wire there was no way she could get out unless she wanted to blow up this whole operation.

Which maybe she did, but I couldn't let that happen.

Not when I was so close to my goal.

"Say something," she whispered.

"I don't have anything to say, siren. It's a hell of a situation."

She wilted a little, as if she'd been hoping I might hold the answer to this riddle.

Her disappointment was unbearable, so even though I had absolutely no reason to do so, I found myself offering, "But you don't have to figure this all out on your own."

"Thanks, Bishop. I . . . I didn't realize how much I needed a friend here. Cross is a dick. Walker, well, he's complicated too. He's just as invested in getting me to stay as his brother, and I don't know who to trust."

"Sterling," I said, swallowing past the lump in my throat.

She blinked those pretty eyes up at me. "What?"

"Call me Sterling. If we're going to be friends, you should probably call me by my first name."

"Sterling Bishop? That's like a fictional super spy name."

I chuckled softly. "So I've been told. My parents were big James Bond fans."

She peered up at me. "And here I thought it had something to do with the color of your eyes."

"That was just a happy accident."

"Could have fooled me, Sterling."

Heat washed down my neck at her use of my name. I'd been Bishop longer than I could remember, but I didn't want to be Bishop with her. Bishop was broken and bloodstained.

He was scarred inside and out. As tarnished as I'd told her she would be if she let Cross get his hooks in her.

Sterling was the man I was supposed to become once upon a time. And maybe, at least in her eyes, I could be him again.

eight

· · ·

River

The rush of water around me muffled all other sounds as I cut through the length of the pool. I needed this. The sensory deprivation swimming offered me was like no other when it came to helping me manage my churning thoughts. Here, I didn't have to be on the lookout for someone who needed something from me, or worse, dangers and distractions that left me destitute. You might say it's my coping mechanism for dealing with the trauma I experienced when I was eighteen.

Before leaving everything I'd ever known to live with my grandmother in Hemlock Harbor, I'd never had this kind of fear. If anything, I'd have said I was fear*less*. Growing up around rugged cowboys, I'd wanted to prove I could do anything they could do, but I also knew beyond all doubt that they'd keep me safe. I'd naively assumed the same would be true in Hemlock Harbor. I couldn't have been more wrong.

Instead of a warm and loving grandma, I'd found an abandoned house and a tombstone. Within twenty-four hours, I'd been mugged, and all that birthday money I'd shoved into my bag was gone. Along with my phone, laptop, and the pretty solitaire necklace my parents had given me only a couple days before.

It had been sink or swim, and I wasn't ashamed to admit that I sank. I sank fucking hard before learning how to swim. Thank God for Bear. If not for him, I may not have survived a week, let alone the ten years I'd managed. He was the one who took me in when I was finally able to call home and found out my parents had been in their accident. Senior had been the one to break the news. He'd also been the one to tell me not to come back until he called me home. Not for any reason. Not even their funeral.

So with nothing left for me in Devil's Grove except heartache and threats and a trust I couldn't access, Bear helped me start over. He also helped me channel all my pain. He gave me a job. Taught me how to defend myself so the next time a punk tried to steal from me, I could fight back. And he offered me a choice between the pool or the ring for dealing with my simmering anger.

Even though I could scrap with the best of them, I'd never been a fan of boxing, so the pool it was. It had been my safe place ever since. Sort of church and meditation and exercise all rolled into one.

I flipped at the end of the pool and pushed off the wall, coming to the surface and turning on my back for a set of backstrokes to cool down. The Cross boys had me tied up in knots. I couldn't stop thinking about that fury-filled kiss in the hallway, the taste of Cross's blood in my mouth, the way he'd ground his hard cock against me even after I bit down on his lip. Meanwhile, Walker, with all his tattoos and bad-boy charm, had starred in a highly inappropriate dream just last night. And then there was Sterling. Wounded. Strong. Supportive. We'd shared a moment outside, one I couldn't deny. He saw me in a way no one else had.

They called to me. All three of them.

And not a single one of them could ever be mine. That's

not why I was here. God, if Gigi heard about this, I'd never hear the end of it. She'd have me in the middle of a cowboy triple-decker sandwich before we ended our phone call.

I'd just completed my lap when a familiar shadow fell across the water.

I pushed my goggles off and squinted up at my visitor. All I could make out was the brawny form and cowboy hat, but backlit as he was, I couldn't place him. That is, not until his amused drawl hit my ears.

"You should'a told me you were going for a swim. I would have joined you, darlin'."

The way Walker said darlin' shouldn't have sent a tingle between my thighs, but it did. Damn him.

He squatted down, those inked forearms of his on beautiful display. With one thick finger, he poked my goggles. "Cute. I especially like the rings they leave around your eyes."

Suddenly embarrassed, I pulled them off and glared at him. "Shut up."

"Make me."

The twinkle in his eyes reminded me of when we were teens and we'd play chicken in this very pool with school friends. We were always teamed up, with me on his shoulders. We'd been the reigning champs. Not quite undefeated, but damn close. Thanks to that one time Cross and his bitchy girlfriend Colleen challenged us. That was the last time we played. I was seventeen and am embarrassed to admit my boobs spilled out of my bikini top as I popped up out of the water. Cross and Walker both saw everything. It was safe to say we didn't play chicken again after that. And I invested in about seven new bathing suits. I'd been a late bloomer and hadn't been prepared for the way everything that had fit at the beginning of the summer didn't by the end.

Guess it was a lesson for all three of us.

"You about done?" Walker asked, pulling me from the memory.

"Yeah, help me out?" I reached for him, but he gave me a dubious glance in response.

"Oh, no. I'm not falling for that. You think I'm new here?"

Well, now that he'd given me the idea . . .

"Are you serious? We're almost thirty years old. I'm not going to pull you in."

He grinned and held out his hand. Trusting fool. The instant our hands were connected, I braced my feet on the side of the pool and tugged with all my might. He went down like a sack of bricks, sending water flying as he windmilled and sputtered.

It was so damn ridiculous I couldn't help but laugh. Even when I caught the promise of retaliation in his turquoise irises.

"This was a brand new pair of boots!"

"Oops. I slipped."

"You . . . Oh, you're gonna get it, ladybug."

"You'll have to catch me first." I was off and swimming for the opposite end of the pool before I finished issuing my challenge.

It may have been a while, but Walker still knew all my tricks, plus he had a few inches on me, and he was able to catch up enough to snag me by the ankle and reel me back.

He pulled me against his chest, wrapping his arms around my waist and holding me tight. "There she is. I keep seeing glimpses of the River I knew."

The lighthearted moment popped, and my smile faded as reality crept back in. "A lot has changed. I'm not that little girl anymore."

His eyes dropped to my cleavage, and his grin curled up. "No, you are not."

I shoved at him. "Walker."

"What? I was agreeing with you." The way his gaze

trailed up to my eyes had my breath catching in my throat. "And in case you haven't noticed, I'm all grown up too."

Swallowing through a tight throat, I nodded. "I gathered that."

"Are you two finished with whatever this is?" Cross's voice was a whip's unexpected lash, making me jump in Walker's hold.

I wriggled free and swam to the ladder, climbing out as Walker continued to stand in the pool. "It's hot. Thought I'd cool off."

"In your clothes?" Cross asked, his focus trained squarely on his brother.

I was thankful. I'd thought nothing of bringing this cheeky bathing suit when I'd packed, envisioning myself spending some downtime at the hotel pool. But now, with most of my ample ass on display in front of the Cross brothers, I was mentally adding a more full-coverage suit to my shopping list.

"Couldn't wait long enough to get my suit on, and I didn't think ladybug would appreciate me going au naturale."

"Still going commando?" I teased, more because I could see how much our playful banter annoyed Cross than because I really wanted to know.

Okay, that might have been a lie. I was a little curious.

Walker winked at me. "You know it, darlin'."

"What did I say about calling me darlin'?"

"That it gets you wet?"

I gaped at him. "I am not wet."

"Sweetheart, you're literally dripping."

"From. The. Pool."

"Keep telling yourself that."

"Walker Wayne!"

He laughed. "River Danielle . . ."

"Jesus fucking Christ. You two are impossible. River, there was an envelope delivered for you by courier. If you're going to order shit, let me know. Tex had to drive out to the gate to meet the delivery guy."

Just that quick, my blood ran cold. "I didn't order anything."

"Well, the mail on your bed says otherwise."

"Wh-who is it from?" I wrapped my towel tighter around my torso.

"How the fuck should I know? I didn't look. You're welcome, by the way."

"God, Danny, you're such a dick," Walker said, climbing out of the pool.

A muscle twitched in Cross's jaw, reminding me that he despised being called Danny. I made a mental note to make sure to call him that as often as possible.

"I've got meetings the rest of the day in Dallas. I'm taking the chopper. I won't be back until morning." He leveled his stare at Walker. "You've got this?"

Got what? Me? The ranch?

Walker gave his brother a two-fingered salute. "All over it."

"Good." Cross turned back toward the house, and as he walked away, I called, "Thanks, Danny!"

His gait faltered, and I could see him clench and unclench his fists.

Score one for me.

Walker snickered. "Vicious, bug. Absolutely vicious."

"Nope. No bug." I tossed him a towel. "I'm not an insect. Also, that's the kind of name you call a kid. As you are well aware, I'm all woman now."

That panty-melting smirk again. God, he was dangerous. "It's that or darlin'. Take your pick."

I shivered, and a knowing gleam entered his eye.

"So what time am I picking you up, *darlin'*?"

"For what?"

"Our date. It's Saturday, and our jailer is away for the evening. Time to go raise a little hell, don't you think?"

As much as I was itching to see what was in the envelope Cross had delivered, I could use a bit of mischief. And mischief with Walker Cross was an experience I never regretted.

nine

Walker

It was a good thing River Adams was my date tonight, because the way she looked in those tight jeans had every cowboy in the bar craning his neck to get a glance at my girl. I could tell she put effort into what she wore, like me. Especially since I saw the bag she arrived with and knew there was no way she hid those boots inside.

"Did you go shopping just for me, darlin'?" I asked, my lips at her ear as I helped her into her chair at the small table we'd chosen.

"For you? No," she smirked. "But you said it was a date, and unless you wanted me to show up in my bathing suit or my PJs, I had to pick some things up."

"Any lacy things on that list?"

"Nothing you'll get to see."

I pouted. "Boo, you're no fun."

"Actually, I'm *lots* of fun. And you think so too, or you wouldn't have run around with me for all those years." She poked me in the chest, and my dick twitched like she'd reached down and given him a tug.

Fuck.

If it was that easy to get me going around her, we'd end

up screwing in the bathroom or the back of my truck before the night was over. Cross would be pissed. I grinned. Sounded like my kind of night.

"So are we drinking or dancing first?"

"What would you say to a shot first?"

She laughed. "Shots? You do realize you're driving, right?"

"I've got someone I can call if things get really wild."

"WILD?" She raised a brow. "Walker Cross, just what do you think is happening tonight?"

"Depends on you. Maybe we'll take the jet to Vegas and come back hitched. What do you say? Wanna be Mrs. Cross?"

Her eyes grew comically wide. "Uh, no thanks. Shotgun weddings aren't really my thing."

"Technically, it's an elopement."

She wrinkled her nose and shook her head. "Either way, hard pass. But as for the shot, it sounds like I'm going to need it."

"What's your poison?"

"Tequila." She started to say something else, but I was already flagging a server down.

"Two . . . make that four shots of Patrón. Silver, if you have it."

"Limes?" the guy asked, barely sparing me a glance.

"Please."

He gave us a nod. "Anything else? If you're gonna order from the kitchen, I'd do it before the band starts. It's about to be a madhouse in here."

"Oh! Who's playing?" River asked.

"Lorde & Wilde. It was a real get for us. These guys are booking out nine months in advance. Tickets sold out for this show in three minutes flat."

River gave me a look, as if asking me how I scored tickets.

I shook my head because, truthfully, I hadn't. My name got me in. Just like it did everywhere else. You didn't turn away a Cross unless you wanted to deal with the fallout.

No one wanted to deal with the fallout. Trust me.

"I'm not hungry," River said with a slight smile.

"You?"

I shook my head, knowing they'd reopen the kitchen if I asked. "Just the drinks for now."

"Be right back," he called, already heading toward the bar.

"So how long have you been planning this?" River asked, narrowing her eyes at me.

"What?"

"This date. It just so happens to fall on the night of a concert. You managed to reserve us a table. Don't think I didn't see the sign when we walked in. Walker Cross, are you trying to seduce me?" She waggled her brows, and I hated thinking she still saw me as the gawky teenager I'd been before she left me.

"That depends. Is it working?"

"Maybe."

"Then maybe."

She laughed. "You're incorrigible."

"Always have been. Always will be."

The waiter arrived with our shots and placed two in front of each of us, along with a small bowl of cut limes. "Anything else, Mr. Cross?"

"Mr. Cross is my grumpy asshole of a brother. Call me Walker." I pulled out my wallet and shook his hand, slipping him a twenty.

The guy gave me a wide grin and took off to a table filled with twenty-somethings looking to score. They were all tits and enormous fake lashes, with so much contour Morticia Addams would be jealous. I silently wished him well, knowing the type and the hangover that accompanied them. No, thank you.

"I'm shocked the famous Mr. Cross didn't go with a fancier label."

"Don't you start. Unless you want me to bend you over my knee and teach you a lesson."

Her eyes darkened, and a flicker of something—was that lust?—flashed in their green depths.

"Besides," I said, speaking over the awkward pause, "everyone knows you don't shoot the good stuff. It's for sipping."

"Oh, everyone, huh?"

"Yes. Any cowboy worth his salt knows what you shoot and what you savor."

Her cheeks went pink, and damn if I didn't have to adjust myself. I hadn't even meant for that to sound dirty, but fuck if my mind wasn't in the gutter now. For the second time in as many minutes, I had to refocus on what we'd been talking about.

Tequila shots. Right.

"You know how to do this, don't you?"

Her lips tipped up in a smug little smile. "Salt, shot, lime."

I hadn't quite known what to expect when I came up with this harebrained scheme. I just knew she was the prettiest fucking woman I'd ever seen, and I'd be damned if I didn't shoot my shot. I wasn't about to make the same mistake twice. Not when fate had seen fit to bring her back to me.

The only Cross who'd have her on his arm was me.

Taking her hand, I brought it to my lip and sucked on the soft spot between her thumb and index finger. Her hitched gasp had me shifting in my seat as I released her and dashed some salt on the wet surface.

"Suck it, darlin'."

Her lips parted, and I swear she was about to ask me what I wanted her to suck.

My dick volunteered. He volunteered so damn fast I could feel the imprint of my zipper down my shaft. I watched with way more interest than I should have as she brought her hand to her mouth and sucked the tender skin. Then, with a spark in her eyes, she tossed back the shot and chased it with the lime.

I itched to take it from her with my teeth, but I held back. She had to make the move this time. She was here under duress, uncomfortable and probably as fucking frustrated as we were.

"You're up," she said with a big smile.

I took her hand in mine again, rewetting and salting the same spot, wanting to get her used to the idea of my mouth being in the same place as hers. Then I tossed back my shot and bit into a lime.

I grinned at her, still holding the green fruit between my teeth. She laughed and shook her head. "You're the most charming cowboy I've ever met, Walker. You know that?"

"Of course I am. And you're the sweetest ladybug I've ever known."

Her cheeks went crimson. "Stop flirting with me."

"Why? This is a date, isn't it?"

She must have seen that as a challenge because she sat up a little straighter and adjusted the bottom of her silk shirt. It was the same color as her eyes and had a big bow where it tied behind her neck. She looked like a fucking present. All I wanted to do was lean over and peel it off her with my teeth. I couldn't even blame the tequila for that one. I'd had the thought as soon as I'd seen her. She was the prettiest thing I'd ever laid eyes on.

"It is. You're right. Okay, flirt away. Give me all you've got, cowboy. Show me what it would be like to be your girl."

Game. Fucking. On.

"Good to know I have the green light. You're up."

This time she didn't wait for me to wet her hand. She leaned in close, and I caught a whiff of her perfume. It was fruity and floral and all her. Before I could do more than acknowledge the thought, her tongue was running up the side of my neck.

Fucking hell, I almost came in my Wranglers.

"Give a guy some warning, darlin'. Not that I'm complaining."

She giggled. "It's a date, isn't it?"

"Damn straight. And in case you're wondering, I intend to kiss you at the end of it."

"Oh yeah?"

"Yeah."

"I intend to let you."

The trickle of salt on my skin had my breath catching. Not because I didn't like it, but because that meant her tongue would follow. I wanted it so bad.

"Go on. Don't leave me like this." Was I fucking begging? Yeah. Yeah, I sure as hell was.

She leaned in a second time, using her tongue to lick up the path of salt. It took everything in me not to wrap my fingers in her hair and slam my lips down on hers. But she was already pulling back, picking up her second shot, downing it, and then claiming mine.

"Hey," I protested, but it was halfhearted at best. Especially when she tossed me a wicked smirk.

With nothing left to do, I claimed the last lime in the bowl and put it between my lips.

Come and get me, darlin'.

It was almost like we were in slow motion as she leaned in and took the lime from me with her teeth. She bit down and sucked the tart juice, then discarded the piece of fruit. When she leaned close once more, her eyes were filled with hunger. I gave in and took her hair exactly as I'd envisioned, tugging hard enough her lips were perfectly positioned for me to kiss.

"Fuck, ladybug," I breathed.

Our mouths collided, and my God, why hadn't we done

Sinner's Secret

this before? She tasted like tequila and limes, but also like my personal fantasies come to life.

"Do we have to stay for the concert?" I whispered against her mouth.

She giggled and linked her fingers behind my head before leaning in for another kiss.

I knew it would be good, but not even my wildest dreams compared to reality. River Adams was my perfect woman. She always had been.

Just as I was about to deepen the kiss, a voice came over the loudspeaker and sent us jumping apart like two teenagers caught neckin' under the bleachers.

"We're thrilled to welcome to the stage, for the very first time here at The Hitchin' Post, Lorde and Wilde. Put your hands together, y'all!"

I didn't let go of her, but we both faced the stage. I might've been a little more reluctant than she was to watch the show now.

"Oh my God, that's Jameson Lorde!"

I registered the words, but my eyes snagged on a familiar face in the corner.

Bishop? It wasn't like our ranch hands didn't get nights off, but what were the odds he'd end up at the same bar as us? What the hell was he doing here, and why was he scowling at me?

River excitedly smacked my arm. "Did you hear me? That's Jameson Lorde! God, I love him. His accent is so sexy."

Jealousy sparked inside me over this Jameson guy, but when he and Killian Wilde took the stage, it was clear as the day was long those two only had eyes for each other.

"Thanks for being here tonight. I'm Killian Wilde, and that tall drink of water is Jameson Lorde, and this is 'London Days, Montana Nights'."

"How could you not tell me we were seeing them? Oh my God, can we meet them after?" She was bouncing in her seat, her grin a mile wide, and suddenly I wasn't jealous at all. I was damn proud of myself for giving her what she wanted without even realizing it.

My life had been a series of dark, reckless acts for longer than I cared to remember. Being with her tonight was like standing in the sunshine for the first time. I hadn't much cared about the family business one way or the other, but knowing that it could taint her, that it would if she stayed here for the full year, had something a lot like guilt twisting me up inside.

She deserved a life in the sunshine, not in the shadows. But that was all I'd be able to give her.

It didn't take long before the audience turned from spectators to dancers, the floor filling with couples, especially during the duo's most romantic ballads. I finally got up the nerve to ask my girl to dance, like a fucking gentleman, and soon she was swaying in my arms. Bishop's attention burned as I pushed her around the dance floor, but I didn't give a shit. She wasn't here with him.

"Did you know your daddy had two sets of books?" she blurted, her words a hair slurred and the accent she'd tried to bury sneaking into her voice.

I stiffened, wondering where the hell that had come from and how she'd found out. "Come again?"

Before she could answer, someone slammed into us, and white-hot pain licked up my side.

I shook it off, offering River a confident grin as I righted myself. But before long, my vision swam, and everything tilted as that initial burn gave way to a deep ache. I staggered into the couple behind us, apologizing weakly as I found my footing and braced myself against a high table. Fuck, something was wrong. My fingers pressed against the source of my pain just as River's gasp caught my ears.

"Walker! Jesus, you're bleeding."

ten

Bishop

I hadn't expected it to be so hard, watching her dance with Walker. But for the first time since, hell, I can't remember when, I wanted it to be me out there. There was no denying the attraction between us. I'd seen it in her eyes out by the swing. Sadly for me, she wasn't an option, not when I had a job to do.

Speaking of...

I cracked my neck and warily eyed the patrons pushing closer to me and my corner table. I'd wanted something that gave me a view of the entire bar but wouldn't allow anyone to sneak up on me. Somewhere I could remain out of sight and out of the way. But I hadn't anticipated a crowd of this magnitude. My mistake. I should've once I saw the name of the band that was playing. It wouldn't have done much, but maybe it would have given me a second to mentally prepare myself for all the jostling.

River swayed in Walker's embrace, her smile bright and a little dazed from the alcohol as he held her close enough no one bothered her. Good man. I had to give him credit. Sure, he'd been crafty about getting a kiss from her, but the guy wouldn't risk her safety by getting sloppy drunk either. He hadn't even tried to order another drink after she stole his. Though I was willing to bet even if she'd allowed him to take his second shot, it wouldn't have done much. He was a big boy. Not as big as me, but then, most weren't.

She said something to him, something he didn't much like if the set of his jaw and stiffness in his shoulders were anything to go by. Then the crowd surged, multiple people moving in all different directions, obscuring my view. Alarm rang through me, causing my heart to pick up speed as I rose and tried to catch sight of them among the sea of cowboy hats.

Instinct drove me from my table when I saw a man slam into Walker's side. Something was wrong. My gut said so. It was too calculated a move, and there was something about the guy that didn't fit in with the crowd despite his Western attire.

It was a hit.

Pushing through the people in my way, I headed straight for Walker and River, my suspicions confirmed when he staggered back and River gasped.

"Walker! Jesus, you're bleeding!"

"Nah, darlin'. I'll be fine. Barely a flesh wound," Walker said, lifting a hand covered in blood. He blanched. "Fuck."

His shirt was soaked, the stain on his side dark and growing by the second. It was bad. Really damn bad. The band was still playing, the people around us oblivious to Walker's dire straits. That worked in our favor for the moment for more reasons than one. We didn't need to create a panic, but we also didn't want to telegraph to whoever did this that they'd failed.

River arrived at the same conclusion because she grappled with her pocket, likely attempting to pull out her cell phone. I stopped her with a hand. Police were the last thing we needed.

"Come with me," I growled.

Her confused green gaze met mine. "Sterling? What are you doing here?"

"What do you think?"

Throwing Walker's arm over my shoulder, I helped him out of the crowded bar, hoping we could just play it off like he was drunk off his ass. Walker was losing blood fast, and his ramblings grew more incoherent by the second.

"Didn't even do anything to earn it this time. No fair," he slurred, his voice weak.

I barely paid him any mind as I scanned the crowd, seeking out other potential threats. I wouldn't hesitate to drop Walker on his ass if I needed to throw River over my shoulder and make a run for it. He'd signed up for this life. She hadn't.

"This time?" River asked. "Jesus, Walker. Do you regularly get shivved on your dates?"

"Only the good ones."

Unlocking my Escalade, I opened the back, thankful I hadn't bothered to put the seats back up.

"Help me lay him down?"

River nodded, eager to help.

Together we managed to get him inside without too much issue. Fucker would still likely cost me an arm and a leg in detailing fees. Blood was a bitch to get out.

Without a word, I ripped open his shirt so I could get eyes on what I was working with.

"Watch where you put your hands, buddy. There's only one person getting into these pants tonight."

"No one is getting in your pants tonight, Walker," River said, her exasperation heavy in her voice.

"Spoilsport." His muttered complaint was cut off by a hiss of pain as he tried to sit up.

"Lie down, you dumbass," I barked.

"Walker, please listen to him. He's trying to help you." Panic had River's pretty features pulled tight as she glanced from me to Walker. "I'll call the ambulance."

"No," both Walker and I said at the same time.

She looked between us. "But . . ."

"9-1-1 means a recording. We don't need to deal with that. If you call anyone, call Cross, but only do that if it looks like I'm dying. You don't want to push that button unless there's no other choice."

"No one's dying. I've got this. Hand me that bag," I told River, jerking my chin toward my field kit.

It didn't take more than a glance to tell the wound was deep and needed to be stitched up. At least it was a relatively clean laceration, the edges of his skin smooth rather than jagged. That would make things easier. I didn't have any sutures with me, but I could probably patch him up enough to get him back to the ranch, where I could deal with the injury properly.

"Well shit, I didn't realize you were a boy scout, Bishop," Walker said, watching me grab what I needed out of my bag.

"Be fucking thankful." I opened a pack of sterile gauze and handed it to River. "Here. I need you to—"

"Apply pressure. I know." She took the gauze with steady hands and pressed hard into Walker's injured side.

The man let out a hoarse cry of agony, but our girl didn't flinch. She was rock solid, unwavering, and more together than I expected. I guess I'd underestimated her.

Sensing my attention, she spared me a brief look. "It's not my first rodeo. My friend Bear—"

"You mean your *boyfriend*?" Walker interrupted with a noticeable sulk.

Boyfriend? Everything inside me protested the new information. There were already two Stetson-wearing obstacles keeping me from her. I didn't want to deal with some Alaskan lumberjack named Bear.

"What? I don't have a . . ." She trailed off, looking a bit guilty. "I forgot I said that."

"Did you lie to piss off my brother?" Walker asked with a chuckle that turned into another hiss.

"Serves him right."

"What about Bear?" I asked, more interested in how she'd become well-versed in emergency triage.

"He's the road captain of the Timberline MC. Those guys can get rowdy, and they have plenty of enemies."

I let out a low whistle. That was a fucking understatement. Their crew was well-known and dangerous. Worry crept through my mind. How the fuck had my siren gotten involved with those guys? I was really at risk of falling into lust with this woman. Hell, I was probably already there. God knew I'd never been so attracted to someone. She was a distraction I couldn't afford.

Unaware of my musings, she lifted one shoulder in a shrug. "Anyway, I've helped clean up my share of the aftermath. Sort of comes with the territory."

"You make a real pretty nurse," Walker said, definitely out of it now.

Shit. He was still losing blood, the gauze River had pressed to his wound already saturated. I passed her two more packets and said, "Keep that pressure. We've gotta get back to the lodge. I need to stitch him up. Keep him awake and talking, siren. You hear me?"

Nodding, she did as I asked, and I bolted for the driver's seat.

"Wait, we can't leave my truck."

"Hush up, Walker. We can send someone to pick it up in the morning."

"But she's my baby."

"And she will still be after you're not bleeding all over the damn place."

I started the car and peeled out of the parking lot, going as fast as I could toward Twisted Cross Ranch. If Cross's baby brother died on my watch, all hell would break loose.

"It was a good thing you were there tonight," River said, talking to me over her shoulder. "What a coincidence."

Yeah. Coincidence.

"Unless you're secretly Walker's bodyguard or something. The two of you make a cute couple."

I wasn't sure who was more offended by her teasing comment.

"I could do so much better than him," Walker protested.

"I'm not his bodyguard."

"So you're just obsessed with me. I get it. I'm irre . . . irrestistible . . . no, that's wrong."

"I think you added a few letters. But you're right. You are irresisible. Tell me more about why Bishop isn't good enough for you."

I barely suppressed the urge to roll my eyes. I knew she was just doing as I'd asked and keeping him talking, but this was a subject I really wasn't interested in.

Still, I couldn't stop myself from muttering, "Who says he's good enough for me?"

"First off, he's too grumpy."

River laughed.

"I get enough of that with Cross."

"Isn't that the truth," she murmured.

"You know, he was never the same after you ran off."

Keeping my eyes on the road, I tuned in to their conversation as much as I could. She didn't need to be mixed up in their shit, but I wondered how embroiled she already was.

"Neither was I."

"Ever think you picked the wrong brother?"

I checked on them in the rearview just in time to see her stiffen before she sighed and whispered, "More than I care to admit."

Walker nodded sagely. "Yeah. I thought . . . think so too. But it's okay, ladybug. I'll give you another shot at me."

River's eyes slid to mine in the mirror. Her cheeks turned bright pink. "Maybe I'm not interested in settling down."

I wasn't sure who those words were for, but they certainly had my attention.

"Your loss. I'm a fucking catch."

"You have to be hard to catch for it to be worth it, Walker," I grumbled.

"Are you slut shaming me?"

"Nope. Just calling it like I see it." I returned my attention to the road. We were maybe another five minutes out from the ranch. Less if I floored it.

"Sterling, the gauze is soaked through. How long until we're there?" River's voice was laced with fear.

I floored it.

"EVERYTHING OKAY IN THERE?" I called, knocking on the bathroom door a few hours later.

The water cut off, and River was still drying her hands when she opened it.

My gaze raked over her, taking in the bloodstained clothes and those haunted eyes. "You should get changed. You're covered in blood."

She swallowed thickly, fighting the tears she'd been trying to keep at bay. "Is he okay?"

I nodded. "He is. He's out now, but I got him all stitched up. Wound's clean. Risk of infection is low, but I'll keep an eye on it. And that ranch hand who met us at the gate, Billy, he already called Cross, who said he's on his way back. I'm sure with his connections, he'll be able to get his hands on any antibiotics his brother might need."

Cross Industries had added a pharmaceutical company to their list of holdings years ago, and Cross Transport and

Freight's two primary products were beef and pills. The legal kind. It was a lucrative move, allowing them to make money from the product and its delivery. It also ensured a level of control most outfits lacked. That meant if Daniel Cross Jr. needed something, he could damn well get it. It also meant he had the means to hide all manner of sins, but that wasn't the point right now.

"Siren? Did you hear me? He's gonna be fine."

She blinked, the stress of the evening taking its toll. "Thank you for taking care of him, Sterling."

"I'd say it was my pleasure, but . . ." I reached out hesitantly, placing a light hand on her shoulder, proud of myself for braving the physical contact. It wasn't so bad when I was the one doing the touching. "You're shaking like a leaf. Come on. Let me walk you to your room."

"Okay, thanks. I just . . . I don't want to leave him."

She cast a look at Walker, asleep in his bed, a little pale but far better than he'd been in the back of the car.

"I promise he's okay. Cross'll be here soon, and the last thing you want is to let him see you like this."

She gave a weak little laugh as she plucked at her ruined shirt. "So much for the new clothes. I'm probably going to have to burn these."

It felt cruel to agree with her, so I just herded her toward the door. I didn't want to give her up, but the truth was tonight had been rough for all of us. There'd be consequences, and if I knew anything about Cross, someone would pay the price for his brother getting hurt.

"Thank you for helping. I mean it," she murmured as her hand went for the doorknob. She paused before turning to face me. "I'm so glad you're here, Sterling."

I was still trying to come up with a response to that when her lips feathered over mine. It happened so fast I wasn't even sure she'd done it except that she froze and blinked up at me.

"Oh my God, I'm so sorry. I don't know why I did that. God, you must think I'm shameless. Catching me kissing both Cross brothers in the same day, although technically, I only really kissed Walker. Cross kissed me, and I bit him—"

I cut off her rambling by taking her chin between my thumb and forefinger and leaning in. "Guess that means it's my turn."

I don't know where the impulse came from, only that the second her mouth hit mine, I needed a real taste. Her lips were soft as velvet and so fucking perfect I never wanted to leave. She sighed into me, her mouth opening just enough to invite me in. My tongue slid inside as I tasted her and deepened our kiss.

It wasn't enough. I needed more. I needed everything.

River lit a fire in me that had long been extinguished. She didn't just make me feel like a man again; she made me feel human. Whole. Unbroken. I'd had to turn off so many parts of myself just to survive that sometimes it seemed like I was barely functioning. But not with her. It made her fucking irresistible. I'd known her less than a handful of days, but I could no more deny the hold she had on me then I could my need to breathe.

She reached up to touch me, and I flinched, breaking our kiss. I fucking flinched and ruined everything. "God, siren, I—"

The front door slammed hard enough the sound echoed through the house as Cross hollered, "River! Walker! Where the fuck is everyone?"

eleven

Cross

"River! Walker! Where the fuck is everyone?" I shouted, the trail of blood leading up the staircase making my gut churn. I swear to God, if Walker died on Bishop's watch, I'd drive that broody asshole to the edge of town and leave his body by the side of the road for the coyotes to dispose of.

I'd just reached the top of the stairs when River and Bishop met up with me. I narrowed my eyes, wondering what they were doing with each other instead of helping my brother, when I caught sight of the blood-soaked shirt clinging to River. It was dry now, but she was covered in it from elbow to thigh.

"Jesus. What the hell happened?" Billy'd told me Walker was hurt bad, not that he'd bled out.

"I thought you knew," River said, her voice more gentle than it'd been since she arrived.

It reminded me of the sweet innocent girl she'd been, and I didn't want to see her like that right now, or fucking ever.

"Knew what? That you two were upstairs doing God knows what while my brother is clearly fighting for his life?"

"Calm down," Bishop snapped, his eyes flashing as he moved, placing his towering frame between her and me.

The guy had a couple inches on me and twenty pounds of solid muscle easy, but with the rage boiling in my veins, not even that would be a match for me. He better watch his fucking mouth before it signed a check his ass couldn't cash.

"In case you've forgotten, Bishop, you work for me. So unless you want to change that, you'd best never tell me to calm down again. Keep your dick away from River and your eyes on your own fucking paper."

"Technically, I work for her."

"Good point. Also, you don't get to decide whose dick goes anywhere near me, thank you very much. You're not my husband or my daddy. And for the record, the only reason Walker is still breathing is because of him, so check your goddamn temper, Cross. Right the hell now. Sterling didn't do anything to deserve it."

Sterling, is it?

I begged to differ. The way that man had been looking at her when they were coming down the hall was evidence enough. He was infatuated. I should know. She seemed to have that effect on men that came anywhere near her. She was practically a bitch in heat, luring every mutt with a functioning dick in range. Including me.

"Look, I stitched up the stab wound, got the bleeding stopped—"

"My brother was fucking stabbed?"

It wouldn't be the first time, but fuck. That meant this wasn't some bar brawl. This was a legit attack. Walker was in someone's sights, which meant *I* was in someone's sights. I was in my father's seat now. You didn't come for one Cross without coming for me too. This was a message. No, a declaration of war.

Motherfucker.

"With some serious rest and fluids, he should be okay. It's

too soon to say for sure that he's out of the woods, but barring infection, he'll be back on his feet in a couple weeks."

Good luck trying to get Walker to stay in bed. I bet my prized stallion he'd be trying to get out of that room by tomorrow afternoon.

"I need to see him."

River stared daggers at me. "He's sleeping."

"Then I'll be quiet. *Sterling*, shall we?"

Bishop didn't acknowledge me. Instead he turned to River. "Go on and get cleaned up, siren. I'll deal with this."

Motherfucking SIREN? The fuck does this guy think he is?

"Yeah, *sparrow*. Be a good girl and do as you're told."

The scoff Bishop didn't even try to hide had my fists clenching. He thought he was going to move in on the woman I'd already fucking claimed? He was wrong. Dead wrong.

River seemed to possess at least an ounce of self-preservation, because she didn't argue. For once. I hated that she was only listening to me because Bishop told her to do it first. I didn't know when they'd gotten so chummy, but she clearly trusted him. It looked like it was time to find a new ranch hand.

Even if this one did come equipped with combat experience and field training.

I watched her go, the sway of her hips in those jeans doing nothing to make me less of a jealous asshole. As soon as she was safely tucked away behind her bedroom door, I turned my attention to Bishop as we walked toward the family wing of the house.

"I don't know what it's been like for you on the other ranches where you've been employed, but here at Twisted Cross, you're expected to keep your dick in your pants, your tongue out of her cunt, and your hands to your goddamned self. Don't make me tell you twice."

I wanted to punch his answering smirk right off his face.

"You sure seem to think that came out as a threat, but to me, it just sounds like a jealous man's challenge. I fucking thrive on challenges."

"Did you know that a crime of passion is a legal defense here in Texas, *Sterling*?"

"Did you know I can kill a man with my bare hands and make it look like natural causes?"

I stared at him.

"What?" He smirked again. "I thought we were exchanging facts, Danny."

I might murder him right here. I could dispose of his body out in the creek. Make it look like he fell and broke his neck. No one would know, and with the way he arrived here, no one would care.

Except maybe River, but some things just couldn't be avoided. She'd get over it. She'd known him what, two days?

I was the one she'd given herself to. I was the one she loved.

You were, until you tore her heart out and handed it to her with a morning-after pill and a break-up note.

I hesitated when we reached the door to Walker's room. For as distant as my brother and I had always been, one thing remained true. We were blood, and that was thicker than water. I had a responsibility to take care of my own—my family and my ranch. Today, I'd failed.

"Did you see who did it?" I asked, putting aside my rampant jealousy.

"No. The crowd was too wild, and I couldn't get eyes on him."

"But it was a man?"

"Absolutely. He disappeared before we even realized Walker'd been stabbed. If the knife had been even an inch to the left, we'd be burying him." Bishop ran a hand over his stubbled jaw. "Hell, if River hadn't kept her cool and applied

Sinner's Secret

pressure all the way home like she did, Walker would be in a hospital fighting for his life."

"I owe you my thanks, then. I won't forget what you did for him."

He dipped his head and turned to walk away.

"Bishop."

A glance over his shoulder was all I got.

"My gratitude doesn't extend to you taking liberties with River. You hear?"

Bishop didn't bother answering. I'd have to make sure he got the message later. Once Walker was in the clear.

I moved into the room, my anger resurfacing as I took in my little brother's pale complexion. Dark circles ringed his eyes, and his chest barely seemed to rise at all. It wasn't all that long ago I'd found my dad in a similar fashion.

Pulling his desk chair close to the bed, I sat down and took his hand, a rare gesture of affection between us.

"Don't you go and try leaving me too. I need you, half-pint. I can't deal with all the vultures circling us on my own. They're fucking everywhere."

I bowed my head and listened to his slow, even breaths, then I pulled my shit together and got to my feet. My phone vibrated in my pocket, ratcheting up my already heightened apprehension.

I pulled it out and glanced down at the screen.

TEX:
We've got a problem, boss.

ME:
What now? I'm busy.

TEX:
Shipment was sabotaged. Product missing. The Russian is pissed.

I clenched my jaw, furious he'd put anything remotely

incriminating in a text, but more worried about what it meant. I hit the call button. He answered on the first ring.

"Never fucking text me again."

"Sorry, boss."

"When did this happen?"

"Couple hours ago? Can't be sure. The driver missed his check-in."

Fuck. That would have been about the same time as Walker's attack. Meaning it wasn't a coincidence, but I needed more information.

"I'll handle it."

I hung up, fuming as I stared down at my brother.

"You want to start a fucking war? You better pray you don't live long enough to meet me, motherfucker, because I'm about to bring it to your doorstep."

With that, I tore out of the room, heading for the one person who could give me more information.

My sparrow.

twelve

...

River

This day was going straight to the top of my emotional whiplash list. Three different men have kissed me; one of them was stabbed, two nearly came to blows, and it wasn't even morning yet. I was exhausted just thinking back to every encounter. And then there was the envelope I had yet to open. The one Cross delivered to my room while I was swimming. I couldn't bring myself to add one more piece of this frustrating puzzle to my already overwhelmed mind. Given its size and weight, I could guess the contents. More pictures. I didn't need those images haunting me either. Not tonight, anyway.

A shower had been just what I needed, at least in terms of a time-out. It was the first time in nearly twenty-four hours that I just got to stop and *be* for a while, aside from my swim. Rifling through my drawers, I pulled out a pair of pajamas I'd gotten on my shopping trip this afternoon. They were soft silky cotton and the least sexy thing I could find.

That distinction seemed necessary. Sort of like battle armor. Although I wasn't sure if it was for Cross or for me. I certainly didn't want to wave a seductive red flag at the bull and agitate him even more.

Tossing my towel on the bed, I reached for the pants, but the door to my room flew open, slamming against the wall and making me drop the pajamas.

"I need you to tell—" he began, but the words seemed to dry up when his eyes landed on me.

"Don't you knock? I'm naked in here." I screeched as I snatched the towel up and hurried to cover my nudity. Cross stood in the doorway, eyes blazing, silent and fuming.

My annoyed outburst seemed to help him find his words. "Do you just stand around without your clothes on? Jesus. Get dressed. I have questions."

"It's my room. I can walk around with my tits out all I want. In fact, Danny, it's my house, so if I decide to stroll through the place in my birthday suit all damn day, I will."

"The hell you will."

I just raised a brow in silent challenge. I had zero desire to parade around naked, but I would be damned before I let this man dictate how I behaved. I'd been in charge of myself and my life since the day I left this town. That wasn't about to change now.

"They're just boobs, Danny. Are you afraid of them?"

"That's not my fucking name, sparrow. You know it."

"Pretty sure it is . . . Danny."

He stormed over to me and flung my PJs in my face.

"Get fucking dressed. This is not a damn joke to me. He almost died tonight, River."

I didn't appreciate the patronizing tone, even if the words did wash over me like a bucket of ice water. "I'm well aware. I was there."

"Which is why I need to talk to you. I need you to tell me everything you can remember about the guy who stabbed my brother."

I stared him down, twirling my finger in the universal signal for *turn the fuck around and stop ogling me, you creep.*

For once, he did as I asked without having to fight me every step of the way.

I started talking as I slid the pants on and then pulled on the long-sleeve button-up shirt. "It happened really fast. I didn't get a good look at the guy. He just sort of bumped into Walker, but I did glance at him because he took off without apologizing."

"Did you see his face?"

"No, just his neck."

"What the fuck good is a neck?"

"Well, smartass, the guy had a tattoo. You can turn around now. I'm done."

He didn't hesitate. He just drilled me with those midnight eyes as he demanded, "What kind of tattoo?"

"It looked like a crying angel. Hands covering her face."

"Motherfucking Russians." The words were low and menacing. "And he didn't touch you? You're okay?"

"Oh, now you're worried about me, *Daniel*? I'm peachy. I never want to do that again, but I'm fine."

"Don't call me that. I'm not my father, and I never want to be him."

"Too late. You're shaping up to be an even bigger dick than he was."

A vein pulsed in his neck, and I realized I'd stepped too far. But if I'd learned anything, I couldn't back down. He'd come in here looking for a fight, and if I showed any sign of weakness, he'd walk all over me. I was not a doormat. I might have been a young girl with a crush once, but I was a grown-ass woman now, and I wouldn't take shit from him or anyone else.

"I was never nice, River. Not even when you thought I was."

"Clearly. Are we done here?" I tried to breeze past him, but he caught my wrist and pulled me back.

"We're not done until I say." He had me up against him,

his height making me feel small as he searched my face for . . . something.

"Let go of me, Cross."

With a bitter laugh, he released me, gaze raking over my pajama-clad body. "Millions at your disposal and you still chose cheap flannel from Target?"

"Yep." I popped the p as hard as I could.

"I liked it better when it was on the floor."

Good God almighty. *We are not turned on by the alpha male asshole, River.* But the state of my pussy said otherwise. She was very responsive to his dickishness. Probably because she could intimately recall how it felt when said dick moved inside her.

"Anything else you feel the need to tell me, Your Highness? Or can I go to sleep now?"

He smirked. "Go on, get between those sheets, sweetheart. I'm glad I'm the last man who got a rise out of you tonight. That means when you slip your fingers between your thighs, it'll be me on your mind."

I glanced purposefully at the bulge beneath his denim. *Well, well, well. Looks like I got a rise out of you too.*

"Joke's on you. I already took care of business in the shower, and it sure as hell wasn't you I was thinking about."

Lies. So many lies.

A muscle in his jaw flexed, but he didn't look away. "I seem to recall you came more than once that night. Your clit was so sensitive and needy. I'm sure you can take care of business a second time. Just remember, when you whisper my name in the dark as you shatter tonight, it's Cross."

It took everything in me not to flick my eyes away from his. But I held fast. "Thanks for the reminder, Danny. Now get the fuck out."

He made a sound that could have been a growl. I could tell he didn't want me to have the last word, but with a curt nod, he finally turned and walked out.

"You could have shut the door behind you, you heathen!" I hollered, stomping over to swing it closed. Then I turned and rested my back against the wall and allowed my eyes to fall closed.

That man was going to be the death of me.

"ARE you sure you're feeling up to this?" I asked, watching Walker as he opened the tack room door.

"C'mon, darlin'. It's been two weeks. I'm practically recovered. Especially with all your tender lovin' care."

Didn't I know it? I'd been at his beck and call ever since our date. Long days spent watching movies together in his bed, playing cards, and, my favorite, reading to each other. I'd enjoyed the time with him, but it hadn't left me with any opportunities to look into Senior's files or test out the list of passwords McCreedy had overnighted to me. I also hadn't worked up the courage to open the envelope from my mysterious pen pal. Thankfully there hadn't been any others, but I knew my grace period was coming to an end. I had to deal with both of those things, and soon. I couldn't forget the real reason I was here.

Unaware of the specter looming over me, Walker tossed me a wink and a smile. "Honest, ladybug. I'm more than up for a ride. It barely even hurts anymore, and I've had worse injuries."

I would have called bullshit, except some doctor Cross had on his payroll swung by this morning and gave him the green light. Two weeks didn't seem like long enough for a stab wound to be fully healed, but it was apparently long enough for him to get back on his feet and resume 'light work.' Whatever that meant. I highly doubted lifting a heavy saddle was considered light.

"Since Cross and Bishop are gone, you ride Hades to get him some exercise."

I still couldn't believe Cross and Bishop had taken off together. A road trip seemed like a terrible idea with the way they'd butted heads, but with Walker out of commission and the way Bishop had proven himself in a crisis, I guess it made a certain sort of sense. Though after the way they'd gone at it, a bigger part of me thought Cross might just be trying to keep Sterling away from me.

"How long has Bishop worked for you?" I asked, loading up everything I needed to get Hades ready to ride.

I didn't miss Walker's grunt of pain as he did the same. The bulky saddle alone was enough to cause strain.

"About a year. He took over when Vic went and got hurt. He couldn't work anymore, so Dad sent him off to be with his family. He's in a better place now."

Something about his intentional use of that phrase gave me the impression there was a bit more to that story. But I wasn't about to push for details.

"Do most of the ranch hands stay a long time?"

"They usually stay for life. We're a family."

I nodded because that was my recollection as well. My dad hadn't had his own ranch; he'd always worked with Senior, but I'd spent enough of my life around cowboys to understand the lifestyle.

Once the horses were ready, we led them out to the trail, the summer heat bearing down on me as intensely as Cross's heated looks always did. I was dressed in cut-off shorts, boots, and a tank top, but Walker wore his Wranglers and a gray T-shirt that did wonderful things for his shoulders. It also showed off his inked arms. I had to admit, I loved watching his muscles as he used the split reins to control Blue.

"Looks like you haven't lost your seat after all these years,

Sinner's Secret

ladybug. I'm impressed." Walker clicked his tongue and urged Blue into a trot. "But can you still race?"

"Walker, I don't think that's a good idea. You're still healing," I called, but he was off, working up to a gallop and not heeding my warning in the slightest.

I knew I couldn't let him go off on his own. If something happened and he reopened the wound or hurt himself, there wouldn't be anyone around to help him. "Goddammit, you stubborn cowboy," I muttered, going after him.

Hades was a massive stallion, powerful and fast as fuck, but I also wasn't used to riding him. He tossed his head, telling me exactly how he felt about having a stranger on his back. I should have eased up and given him time to get accustomed to me, but Walker was playing with fire. His stitches had only just come out, and the idiot was acting like he hadn't been attacked a few weeks ago.

Centering myself, I worked Hades into a steady lope, the two of us eating up the space between Walker and me. This was as close to flying as I'd ever get, and I'd forgotten how much I loved the feel of the wind whipping my face as we raced across the land. I closed in on Walker, who was approaching the creek, his horse already in position to jump. Jesus, he really was going to hurt himself again. I sure as hell couldn't lift him.

I held my breath as he and Blue leapt across the moving water as if they'd done it a hundred times before. Which they had. A shuddering laugh escaped me. It seemed silly to be so worked up. Walker'd been riding nearly as long as he'd been walking. He knew what he was doing, yet I couldn't shake the anxiety skating beneath my skin.

"C'mon, fraidy cat. You know how to jump. What are you waiting for?" he called, amusement and elation in his voice.

He was so in his element out here, living the cowboy life, being with his horse and on his land. It lightened something in my heart I hadn't realized had been weighing so heavily.

Leaning forward, I patted Hades on the neck and whispered, "Okay, boy, I know you can do this. Let's get him. Don't let me down."

There was no way in hell I'd leave Walker on the other side of that creek, because if it didn't happen now, it was going to later. He'd need me eventually.

"I'm coming. Keep your shirt on."

"Are you sure? I have a sexy new scar I can show off." He grinned as he reached for the hem of his T-shirt.

Digging my heels into Hades's side, I pushed him forward. We flew down the hill, and it took everything in me not to close my eyes as we made the jump. Remembering my years of training, I moved with the horse, and we landed gracefully on the other side, exhilaration rushing through me and leaving me breathless.

"Holy shit!" I said, wide-eyed as I looked at Walker, who just smiled proudly. "That was a fucking rush."

"Isn't it? It's good to see my ladybug is back. I really missed you."

"Missed me? I've barely left your side in weeks."

"Yeah, but"—he gestured to the expansive wilderness all around us—"not out here where we belong."

We were miles away from the lodge with no people in sight, just the two of us and our horses, blissfully alone together. Until right now, the thought of not having help available had sent fear through me, but I'd been wrong. He was fine. He knew his body and what he was capable of.

"Follow me, darlin'. I want to show you something."

He clicked his tongue again and took his horse up the slight hill. I followed, excited at the prospect of a surprise, but as I directed Hades to trail after Walker, the horse stamped his foot and began backing away, acting erratic and fearful. Shit.

"Whoa, there," I said, tone easy and calm even though I was feeling anything but.

It was too late. Hades let out a whinny of fear and reared

back, throwing me onto the stone-covered creek shore. Pain radiated through my hip and shoulder where I collided with river rocks, and the horse bolted.

"Fuck, you asshole horse. You and Cross deserve each other! What was that about?" I sat up, assessing myself for injuries. I was sore and would likely be covered in bruises, nothing was broken.

Before I could get to my feet, I heard Walker call my name and the sound of Blue's hoofbeats as he approached.

"I'm okay! Hades is gone. Can you help me up there with you?"

He appeared over the ridge, eyes hard and narrowed on me with fury.

But he wasn't here to help me. Walker Cross pulled a gun from his side holster and trained it on me. "Don't fucking move."

thirteen

Walker

*J*esus fucking Christ. River didn't even see the rattler coiled and ready to strike behind her. It was just out of range, but if she moved, she'd likely end up bit.

I cocked my gun, and River's eyes flared. "Walker, w-wait—"

Not waiting for her to finish, I squeezed the trigger, splitting the fucking snake in two.

She was curled in on herself, hands covering her face protectively, eyes shut tight. But as the echo of the gunshot faded, she carefully removed one hand and opened first one, then both of her eyes. Her fear morphed into relief that quickly turned into outrage.

"What the hell, Walker? You shot at me!"

"I did fucking not."

"Did too."

"Are you shot?"

She looked down, assessing herself. "No, but only because you missed."

I shook my head. "Darlin', I don't miss." Then I holstered

my gun and gestured at the remains of the snake behind her. "Exhibit A."

"Fuck!" she shouted, jumping away.

"A little late for that, don't you think?"

"I guess that explains the horse," she muttered, gingerly standing up and rubbing at her ass.

"Are you okay?"

She wasn't okay, but I had to ask rather than assume, because if I just started taking care of her, she'd push back and pretend it was fine.

"I really thought you were going to kill me," she admitted as she climbed the hill.

I reached down and gave her a helping hand, but she winced, clearly favoring her shoulder.

"Why would I kill you? Are you serious?"

She stood a few feet away, dirty, sweaty, and so damn pretty my chest hurt. "I think it's a reasonable reaction to someone pointing a gun at you, Walker."

"You really have been gone too long. You know there are snakes out here. I'm pretty sure Texas is where Disney got the idea for that line."

"Uh, they write lots of lines. You might need to be more specific."

I rolled my eyes. "Oh, come on, they only have one cowboy."

She wrinkled her nose, looking confused. "Mmm, nope, still not ringing a bell. You're just going to have to spit it out."

"You know the one, 'There's a snake in my boot.'"

It wasn't until the first giggle escaped that I realized she'd been playing with me. "You little shit," I grumbled half-heartedly.

Dismounting, I held the reins and brought Blue closer to River, knowing I'd have to help my girl up on the horse.

"We should go back. I think I've had enough ranching for

the day." She offered me a weak smile. "I forgot about the snakes. That was stupid."

"Bound to happen when you become a city slicker."

She laughed, but there was no humor to it. "I moved to a small town in Alaska. We barely have a CVS and don't even mention Target. I went without for so long."

"Ah, the two carts' worth of stuff you bought on your shopping trip makes so much sense now. C'mon, let's get you on this horse so we can head home."

I bent over and offered my threaded fingers for her to use as a step so she could easily mount. The site of my stab wound pulled and throbbed, reminding me I was overdoing it, but I'd be damned if I let her see my pain.

Once she was seated, I joined her, grunting against the sharp stab running through my side.

"You good?" I asked, taking the reins with one hand and wrapping my other arm around her waist to help keep her secure. That was my story, and I was sticking to it.

"Maybe? I don't know. My hip hurts in this position. Is there somewhere we can rest for a little while?"

Shit. She was tense, her shoulders hunched like she was protecting herself.

"Yeah, there's a cabin not far from here. We can go there."

All across our land, we'd put in first aid shelters. We got wild storms out here, and with the number of people who worked the ranch, we needed safe places for them to care for injuries, fucking snake bites, or to just hunker down and wait out dangerous weather. It'd been Cross's idea after we lost one of our best hands to a rattlesnake bite. Emergency services hadn't been able to get to him quick enough. Cross was convinced if he'd just been able to get to a dose of antivenom, we would have been able to save him.

This was the first time I'd needed to make use of one, though, and I had to admit I was thankful I had an option at the ready for her. I didn't love the idea of forcing her to suffer through the pain longer than absolutely necessary. We were looking at a two-hour ride at minimum with both of us on Blue. I couldn't willingly put her through that when we'd be at the cabin in ten minutes, maybe less.

It took seven minutes. The pain in my side was worse with every step Blue took, so I was thankful as fuck when I was able to dismount. I had to clench my teeth to keep from whimpering as I helped River down, but she noticed.

"Are you hurting?"

"Just a bit. I'll be fine."

"I knew this was a bad idea."

"Yeah, but I got to have your ass pressed up against me for that part of the ride, so I'd say it was worth a little pain."

She rolled her eyes and sighed. "Don't you go trying to make lemonade out of lemons. I almost got bit by a snake, we're both hurt, and my horse abandoned me."

"Cross's horse."

"Like horse like rider," she muttered with so much bitterness I knew she was referring to something specific.

"What was that?"

"Nothing."

"Let me put Blue away, then we need to look at your side. Go on in. It should be unlocked."

I hobbled to the small stable and got my horse taken care of, a sweat breaking out on my brow as I hefted the saddle. Shit. I'd done a number on myself. I was gonna be spending alone time with the woman of my dreams, and I'd be useless to her if this kept up.

River

Sinner's Secret

WALKER CAME in as I was standing in front of the mirror in the small bathroom. I'd tugged my shorts down to inspect the damage on my side. My leg was a little scraped up, but most of the fall had been broken by my shoulder and hip. A bruise was already blossoming across my skin. God, I was going to be so sore.

I startled as Walker let out a low whistle, my eyes flying to find his in the mirror.

"That looks rough."

"Hades is a big horse. It was a long way down. I'm lucky nothing's broken."

He nodded, moving closer and gently running his fingers over the bruise. I shivered, but it had nothing to do with pain.

"I think we have some arnica in the first aid kit. I'll grab it for you so you can rub it in after you get out of the shower. Towels and stuff should be in there." He gestured with his chin to the little cabinet hanging over the toilet. "Not sure we've got any spare clothes in your size, but I'll see if I can rustle something up for you so you don't have to put your tore up shirt back on."

"Thanks, Walk. What about you? Is your side okay?"

With his signature cocky grin, he lifted his shirt, displaying washboard abs and a deep red scar on his side. The faint dots from where the stitches had gone in were still visible. But it wasn't reopened or bleeding, and the edges didn't seem inflamed.

"It's just tender. I'm fine. Don't worry, ladybug, I'm not gonna drop dead on you."

A relieved sigh escaped me before he shot me a wink and left.

My shower was equal parts wonderful and awful. The scrapes stung where the water hit, but the feeling of getting clean after being such a mess made up for it. As did the way the muscles in my back loosened under the heat and pressure of the water cascading on them. Thank God for rich cowboys, or this would've been a no water heater situation.

A dark gray shirt was folded and waiting for me on the counter. I toweled off, wincing as my muscles pulled and stretched. The next few days were going to suck, but at least I didn't have to ride back to the main house just yet.

I took a look at my bra and panties, and everything in me protested. Not just at putting on soiled clothes, but the twisting required to wrangle myself into them. I needed some time to work up to that task. The shirt slipped on easily, falling to mid-thigh and covering the important bits. Walker wouldn't mind.

He was barefoot and shirtless when I exited the bathroom, his cut physique on perfect display as he worked some kind of cream into his fresh scar.

My mouth went dry, and I'm pretty sure he caught my dumbfounded expression when he glanced up at me.

"See something you like, darlin'?"

I blinked and reached for the unaffected mask I usually reserved for his brother. "I was just trying to work out why you're the one with his shirt off when I'm the one who took a shower. I've heard of sympathy pains, but sympathy nudity? That seems like a stretch."

"You could join me. Take your shirt off, and then we'd be even."

I crossed my arms. "Ha ha. Very funny."

"Nothin' I haven't seen before," he taunted, reminding me of that time we'd thought it'd be a good idea to go skinny dipping. Still, I was a whole lot more grown now.

"That's not . . . this is . . . we—" This was impossible. He was like Cross, but the sweetest, most flirty, and caring version.

The Cross brothers were my catnip, and even if I hated the eldest, I just wanted to roll around in them and let them pet me. Was this what they called being a glutton for punishment?

"You're pretty when you blush, ladybug."

"And you're a lot smoother than I remember, *Woody*."

"Come on over here, and I'll show you a woody you'll never forget."

I gaped and then laughed. "You did not just say that with a straight face, Walker Wayne."

"Sure did. But seriously, come over here so I can put this cream on your bruises. It'll help. Promise."

More than a little aware of my undergarment situation, or lack thereof, I shook my head and held out my hand. "Nuh-uh, I'll do it."

He rolled his eyes and slapped my hand away. "Stop being so stubborn. I'll behave myself."

"I'm . . . I'm not wearing anything under the shirt."

Heat blazed to life in his irises. "Is that so?" His lips twitched upward. "Now why is that?"

"They seemed too hard to put on. All the reaching and stretching."

"Which only proves my point. Turn around and face the wall. I promise I won't try to cop a feel or nothing."

What if I want you to?

Shit, where had that thought come from?

I turned away from him, my heart pounding as the anticipation of his touch built to nearly unbearable heights. With one hand, he slowly lifted the back of my borrowed T-shirt. The air felt overly cool against my exposed skin, but so far, Walker was true to his word. Other than a slight hitch in his breath, he didn't make any comment about what he'd just revealed.

His fingers were warm and tender as he massaged the arnica into my flesh, being so careful not to hurt me.

"This is going to be sore for a few days, darlin'," he whispered, his voice tight as his touch disappeared from my hip. "Where else do you hurt?"

I had to clear my throat before I could get my words out. "My shoulder."

He didn't hesitate, sliding that T-shirt up higher. "Is this okay? We'll have to take the shirt off so I can get to it."

Biting down on my lower lip, I nodded.

"Arms up, pretty girl."

I obeyed, my pulse picking up as he pulled my shirt over my head. He handed it to me, saying, "So you can cover up." But he stayed behind me, still behaving. For now, anyway. And to be honest, I wasn't sure I wanted him to be the good guy anymore.

"Your hip took the most damage, but let's make sure that shoulder is taken care of too." Goosebumps broke out across my whole body as he massaged my back and shoulder blade, then worked his fingers across my ribs, accidentally brushing the side of my breast as he ran them over my sensitive skin.

I moaned involuntarily, and he responded with a low hum.

"Make another sound like that, and I'll lose what little control I have left. I'm walking a thin line now that my hands are on you."

I should put a stop to this. I already had a complicated history with one brother; I didn't need to add the other one to my collection and make an even bigger mess out of things.

It had been weeks since my last encounter with Cross or Bishop, but that didn't diminish my attraction to them. I'd resolved to shut down my vagina's need to make nice with their dicks, but Walker and I had a connection. There was no doubt about it. We had chemistry in spades.

"Walker, I . . . Cross kissed me."

His fingers stilled, a soft curse rushing across my ear.

"And I kissed Bishop as well. I just really needed you to

know that. I'm a fucking mess. You don't want to cross this line with me. I don't want to hurt you."

"I'm a big boy. I can handle a little healthy competition. I've been waiting in the wings for you a long time, River. Cross can either step up to the plate or fall back and let me take my shot." His lips feathered over my nape, driving me near to distraction.

"W-what about Bishop?" The question was little more than a breathy whisper, but I needed all my cards on the table before this went any further. I might be selfish, but I wasn't out to hurt anybody.

"I stood aside so you could have what you wanted once, and I lost you because of it. I'm never going to step aside again. If Bishop wants you, he'll have to take you from me."

I took a ragged breath before dropping the shirt. Then I leaned my head back against his chest and took his hands slowly moving them from where he'd rested them on my waist. I guided him around until he was cupping the weight of my breasts and whispered, "If you're going to touch me, Walker, then *really* do it."

I could feel his smirk against my skin. "Does this mean I don't have to behave anymore?"

fourteen

Walker

Never in my wildest dreams did I think I'd have River Adams naked and at my disposal. Okay, maybe my *wildest*. Her skin was warm and soft, and those tits fit perfectly in my palms.

"Are you up for this, darlin'? I know you're hurting."

"No more than you."

"How 'bout this. We go real slow, and if anything feels less than in-fucking-credible, you say the word, and we put a pin in it for today?"

She nodded, slowly turning to face me, showing me her gorgeous curves. Goddamn, I could write a sonnet about the teardrop shape of her breasts, not to mention the full swell of her hips and those long, toned legs that just seemed to go on for miles. Even banged up as she was, I wouldn't change a damn thing.

"Kiss me," she demanded, her hands moving to my belt and working it open.

"Yes, ma'am." I lowered my head and swept my lips across hers, teasing and tasting the woman I'd wanted since I figured out I liked girls.

She parted her lips, inviting my tongue inside. I wasn't

one to leave a woman wanting. My fingers slid into her hair, pulling the tie out and letting those tresses fall free so I could grip them.

"You're mine now, darlin'. You understand? Once we do this, I won't be able to keep from wanting you."

"Were you able to before? It's been my experience that once I want someone, that never goes away, even if I don't act on it."

I shoulda known she'd call my bluff. She'd always known me better than anyone else. Just like I did her. Which is why I knew better than to ask who she was still thinking about all these years later.

I already knew the answer; it'd been in her eyes the second they'd landed on my brother. Difference was, this time I didn't give a shit. Life was too short not to grab the bull by the horns.

"You can want him and still have me. It doesn't change how I feel, ladybug."

"And how's that?" she whispered, her lips moving over mine in the imitation of a kiss as she worked me free of my pants.

"Head over fucking heels, baby. You're it for me. You always have been."

I needed her so damn bad. My cock ached from how hard she made me. Tilting her face up, I kissed her again as I slid my hands down her arms until I could twine our fingers together.

"I'm not fucking you for the first time against a wall."

"What's wrong with the wall?" she asked, shoving my pants to the ground.

The way she eyed my cock had me swallowing a groan.

"Let's save the wall for when we're both a hundred percent." I led her to the only remaining door in the cabin. "The bedroom's back here."

Her fingers played along the ridge of my cock until she reached the first of four metal balls.

"A piercing, huh?"

"Two, technically."

"And what's this fanciness called?"

"You asking if my dick has a name, darlin'?"

She gave me an exasperated look before tracing a line from one barbell to the next. "The piercing. I've heard of a Prince Albert, but I don't think this is the same thing."

It was hard to breathe around the wave of sensations her touch sent crashing through me. "Magic cross."

"How appropriate."

"Not gonna lie," I gritted out as she continued exploring me. "That was part of the appeal."

"Are you magic, Walker Cross?"

"Only one way to find out, darlin'. Get your ass on the bed."

Her ass was the perfect heart shape as she crawled onto the bed, and I had to bite back a groan at the sight of her glistening pussy peeking out from between her thighs. I wanted to taste her and get her to grind that pretty cunt against my mouth.

When she started to twist, I halted the movement with a hand on her ankle. "No, you're perfect just like this. All you need to do is spread your legs a little wider for me."

She did, opening herself up as I sank to my knees next to the bed, putting my face in direct range of my target.

"Walker . . ."

"Shh, I've been waiting what feels like my whole damn life for this moment. Let me enjoy it."

"Please," she stuttered out when I still hadn't done more than blow a line of hot air down her slick seam.

She tensed as I buried my face in her pussy, lapping at her and loving how wet she already was for me. Her desperate cries began as soon as I found her clit, and without prompting, the woman started riding my face like I was a bucking bronc she wanted to break.

"Fuck yeah, darlin'. Use me. Get yourself off with my mouth."

"Jesus, Walker."

Her release came fast and hard, the rush of slick sweetness coating my tongue and making my balls draw up tight. I would not come all over myself without getting inside her. I backed away, my hands skating over the backs of her thighs as I got to my feet. My dick twitched, the need to fill her overwhelming.

"The condom's in my jeans," I grumbled. "I'll be right back."

"I'm on the pill, and I haven't been with anyone in a long time."

The way she trusted me with her body and her safety made pride swell inside me. "I was tested recently. I won't give you anything."

"Then what are you waiting for, Walker? Please. I want you."

A little warning came to life in the back of my mind, though. My dad always told us to wrap it up unless we wanted to get saddled with a surprise. He didn't trust that women who were with a Cross man for a night weren't just trying to get a free ride in the form of child support. But that wasn't River. She didn't need to take us for all we had. She'd already been given the keys to our kingdom.

Smoothing a palm down her back, I positioned her a bit closer to the edge of the bed.

"I'm gonna have to go slow. Tell me if it hurts, okay?"

She nodded and looked back over her shoulder. "You too, cowboy."

I wasn't too worried about that being an issue. The ache in my side was nothing compared to the ache in my balls.

Holding her hips steady, I ran the swollen tip of my cock through her folds, making us both groan.

"More. Please, I need more."

I pressed inside, agonizingly slowly, with a level of control I honestly never thought I possessed. It felt like it took an entire minute for me to finally bury myself inside her. We were both shaking by the time I bottomed out. I'd thought going slow would make it easier for me to last. I was so fucking wrong. Her tight walls were hot and smooth, squeezing every inch of me and testing my willpower like no other.

All I wanted was to pull out and slam back in, rock into her as fast and hard as I could. But the bruises on her body and the wound in my side dictated how wild things could get for us. This time, I was making love to her, slow, deep, and intense.

"Hand between your legs, River. Give that clit what she needs."

She reached down and touched herself until her breaths came in shallow gasps, and I rolled my cock inside her in mesmerizing waves. I needed her to come all over me so I could follow.

"Walker. I'm close."

"Fuck, yes, darlin'. Get yourself off on me." I gripped her unblemished side and let myself drive in a little harder, just until my scar reminded me it was there. "I'm fucking close too."

My balls pulled tight as her walls clamped down on me, and she cried out my name like she was lost and I was her saving grace.

"That's my girl. You take my dick so good. Goddamn, you feel like a dream squeezing my cock like that."

I gave her one final slow thrust to see her through the last of her climax before I pulled out and fisted myself. She'd lubed me up better than any bottle as I shuttled my hand up and down my shaft a couple of times, and then I was spurting ropes of cum all over her sweet ass and spine.

My heart finally slowed after a few moments of euphoria, and I reached down to trail my fingers through my cum, writing my name on her skin.

"You're gonna need another shower," I murmured.

She made a sleepy sound I thought was agreement. "After a little nap."

"Wore you out, did I?" I snagged a couple of tissues from the bedside table and cleaned her up before the two of us collapsed together on the bed.

Snuggling into me, she sighed. "You were right. It is magic."

fifteen

Cross

"Something's not right."

I knew it before Bishop said a word as I pulled my F-150 around to the barn. Five ranch hands sat atop their horses, all talking together with serious expressions on their faces.

"I told you we shouldn't have gone this time. We should've waited it out a few more days," Bishop grumbled.

I gritted my teeth against the retort that wanted to be freed. It wouldn't do any good. He was right anyway. Despite a handful of covert surveillance missions, we hadn't found a damn thing. Just dead ends and cold trails.

I thought for sure we'd get a hit this time. It was the same route as the last tainted shipment and the same driver. But someone must have tipped them off because it was textbook from start to finish.

"I think we have a rat," I said, more to myself than anything.

Bishop grunted in agreement. The big fuck didn't speak much most days, but even less since we'd gotten near home. You'd think that would make him a shit road trip companion, but I appreciated the quiet. Gave me time to think.

My reasoning for bringing him with me might have started off petty, but he'd proven himself an asset. Not just as a stand-in for my brother, but because he was perceptive. Spotting things I know for a fact others would have missed or written off. And he'd already proven himself useful in a fight. It was always good having guys around who weren't afraid to get their hands bloody. He kept this up, I might have to talk to Walker about offering him something more permanent.

It was just a bonus that going on these runs with me kept him far the fuck away from River.

"Go check that out, will ya? I need to talk to Walker." I didn't give him a chance to answer as I stormed toward the house, calling Walker's name.

When he didn't answer, unease skittered down my skin. Anger replaced it almost immediately as I shoved open his door and found his room empty. So I went tearing down the hall, one woman on my mind. The one who was supposed to be taking care of him.

"Sparrow?"

Prickles walked across my neck when she didn't answer either. "Goddammit, River. I'm not playing. Where the fuck are you?"

I'd already set off toward my father's office since that's where she spent most of her mornings, but Bishop's terse shout stopped me in my tracks.

"Cross?"

"I told you to deal with it, Bishop. I'm in the middle of something."

"They're gone."

My spine straightened as I stared him down. "What do you mean, gone?"

"I mean, gone. No one's seen them since yesterday. Walker's horse is gone too."

"The ranch hands . . ." I started, my brain piecing together what we'd seen when we arrived.

"Found your horse saddled and without a rider a couple miles due east of here. Hades was heading back on his own."

My initial worry that Walker'd taken River and run off vanished at that piece of information. A horse with no rider meant only one thing. Someone had been thrown, possibly hurt.

I raced back down the stairs and out the front door, barking orders to anyone who'd listen.

"Saddle my damn horse," I growled at the nearest hand, a young guy who hadn't been part of the ranch long. I knew his name, though. I knew all their names. This one was Tommy. His daddy had been one of our most loyal, and when we'd lost him in a deal gone bad, we'd promised his mama he'd be taken care of.

"Did anyone think to check the cabins?" I snapped at Tex as I burst into the barn.

"We've already got guys on it."

"They have their radios?"

"O'course."

"Check in. I want to be the first to know when my brother's found."

"You got it, boss."

Tex was already talking into his walkie when Tommy appeared with Hades in tow, the big stallion huffing his annoyance at being forced out of his stall.

"Too bad, old man," I murmured, taking the reins from Tommy and patting my horse's neck.

Hoofbeats behind me called my attention away from Hades and to the rider approaching. Bishop sat on his white horse, appropriately named Ghost.

"Go check the creek. If Walker's trying to get in her pants, he might've taken her to camp out there," I told him as I mounted Hades and adjusted the reins.

"No."

"Excuse me?"

"Respectfully, no. I'm with you. If they're hurt, you'll need help."

"Respectfully, fuck you."

"Think about it. You can't ride back with three people on one horse. If something happened to them, you'll appreciate the extra set of hands."

I huffed out a frustrated breath, not used to needing to rely on anybody and fucking hating it. Until Dad died, I was the enforcer. I told everyone else what to do. And if they couldn't get it done, I took care of it myself.

"Like it or not, I'm coming with you. Last I heard, River was the boss. Not you."

"If you were trying to win me over, that was the exact wrong way to go about it."

He shrugged. "Way I figure, I saved your brother's life, so I'm already ahead."

I didn't have time for this. Not if they were in a bad way. I'd seen men die out on this ranch because no one got to them in time.

"Fine. But stay out of my fucking way."

I clicked my tongue and kicked my heels into Hades's sides until he took off, building speed until we were galloping back in the direction the others had found him.

We rode for the better part of an hour, searching for any trace of River or my brother. Frustration burned through me as we reached the hill's crest that looked over the creek. The rocks on the other side were stained a rust red, and my blood ran cold at the sight.

"I've got something," I called, but Bishop was already jumping the creek.

"Someone blew this snake's head clean off."

Snake? Shit.

Every possible scenario raced through my head, all of

them ugly. If either of them had been bit, the only place they could've gone was the nearby cabin.

The walkie I'd grabbed came to life with a crackle, Tex's voice tinny and static laced coming over the line.

"Blue is in the stable at cabin 7, boss. Want me to send the guys in?"

"No. I'm ten minutes out. I'll be right there."

"Copy that."

I didn't even look at Bishop. I simply clicked my tongue and urged Hades into a run, one goal in mind. Make sure my sparrow was okay. And if I found out she was, there'd be hell to pay for scaring the shit out of me.

It wasn't long before the cabin came into view, and just as promised, my brother's horse was in the stall we'd erected outside.

"Motherfucker."

Even though my adrenaline was pumping, the extra miles had given me some time to think. If someone was really hurt, the other would have called for help by now. Even if their cells were dead, the cabin had a landline and spare walkie for this exact reason.

Those two weren't injured.

I dismounted, secured Hades to the hitching post, and tore up the steps leading to the front door.

Did I knock? The fuck I did. I tried the handle but found it locked. No. He did not get to make us all worry then take her out here and fuck her like one of his buckle bunnies.

I didn't bother to investigate why the thought of them together pissed me off so much. Instead, I used my fury as fuel and kicked the damn door in.

Walker was standing in the doorway to the bedroom, surprise flickering across his face. His jeans were half done up, his hair a mess, hickeys on his neck and bare chest.

"What the fuck, Cross?"

"Don't you what the fuck me. Where is she?" I stormed

inside, got right in his face, and had to force myself not to push him into the doorframe.

Walker wasn't afraid of me, though. He puffed up like a damn peacock and squared off with me. "She's in the shower. She needed one after last night."

A low, angry growl sounded deep in my throat. "The fuck do you think you're doing, Walker? She is not a goddamn game."

"Who said I was playing a game?"

"Your behavior, for one. Do you have any idea how irresponsible it is for you to run off without anyone knowing where you are? In case you haven't realized it yet, we're one fuckup away from a full-blown war with the Russians."

"Why don't you say what you really mean, Cross? I'm the fuckup. Right? Because, of course, my being here is just another in a long line of fuckups. Since I'm so irresponsible and all. I couldn't possibly be up to any good."

"You call spending the night with your face in her cunt doing good? I can smell her all over you."

"So that's what this is about." Walker smirked, but it was mean. "You're just jealous she chose me over you. Well, too fuckin' bad, you had your chance and blew it. For once, you can be the spare."

"That really gets your goat, doesn't it? That I'm the heir apparent. You're so self-conscious you never got over those rumors. Pathetic."

"I'm pathetic? You're the one throwing a goddamn tantrum 'cause I fucked your girl."

"She's not my anything." The lie burned in my gut, but I ignored it.

"Is that so?"

"If she's anything, she's my sloppy seconds. A stray that needs to be thrown out. We agreed. She cannot stay here. She'll ruin everything. She's already putting her nose where it doesn't belong."

Some of the fight left my brother. "She knows about the books."

Fuck.

"I'll deal with it."

"But—"

"I mean it. She's off-limits, Walker."

"You told me to handle her."

"I said distract her, not fuck her."

A soft gasp from behind me had me spinning toward the bathroom. My eyes clashed with River's, and the devastation I saw in those green depths wrecked me.

Fuck.

For one brief moment, I wished I could walk it all back and keep from hurting her. The apology was on the tip of my tongue, but I swallowed it, standing up straighter and slipping on my cold mask of indifference instead.

Nothing had changed. She was never mine to keep. My world would chew her up and spit her out. The only way to keep her whole was to be the reason she walked away.

It was better if she hated me. This would be so much easier if she did.

sixteen

River

 I'd never been with a guy who was pierced before. It was possibly my new favorite accessory. I was deliciously sore, and it had nothing to do with the bruises along my shoulder and hip. After the first round, Walker had gone down on me again, forcing me to come on his tongue over and over until my voice was raspy from screaming his name.

I'm not sure what time we fell asleep, but he'd woken me up near dawn as he slowly thrust inside me. And then he made love to me once more, just as slowly and carefully as the first time, but no less intense.

How had I missed him back when we were kids? He was so much better for me than his brother. Walker was everything Cross wasn't. Kind, caring, honest. He didn't use people or play games with their hearts.

I bit my lower lip as I ran my fingers over the beard burn on my inner thighs. Maybe he'd go for one more round before we went back?

Shutting off the water, I was ready to waltz into the bedroom naked to present the idea but stopped with my hand on the doorknob at the sound of raised voices. Not sure what

I was about to walk into, I wrapped myself in a towel and cracked open the door.

"I'm pathetic? You're the one throwing a goddamn tantrum 'cause I fucked your girl."

"She's not my anything." Cross's voice was cold and detached, as usual, but it didn't hurt any less.

"Is that so?"

"If she's anything, she's my sloppy seconds. A stray that needs to be thrown out. We agreed. She cannot stay here. She'll ruin everything. She's already putting her nose where it doesn't belong."

Anger lit a fire in my heart at his coarse words. I tightened the towel, ready to rush out there and show a united front with Walker. But then the man I'd just spent the night with spoke, and my world crashed to the ground.

"She knows about the books."

"I'll deal with it."

"But—"

"I mean it. She's off-limits, Walker."

"You told me to handle her."

"I said distract her, not fuck her."

Any part of my heart that Cross hadn't broken ten years ago shattered.

"You slimy sonofabitch!"

Cross's gaze found me first, and something that couldn't possibly be regret flashed in his eyes before his usual cool mask fell into place. Walker spun toward me, his expression stricken.

"River, I—"

"Save it. You've said more than enough."

Walker reached for me, but I flinched away.

"Ladybug, I'm so—"

"You know, I thought Cross was the asshole in the family, but I was wrong. At least he's been honest about what a fucking dick he is. You . . . you're worse than he ever was."

My voice cracked on the last sentence, only fueling my fury. The Cross boys didn't deserve my tears or my heartbreak.

"Enough," Cross barked. "River, get dressed and get your ass on my horse. We'll deal with this at the lodge."

"The fuck I will."

"You do not want to push me right now, sparrow."

"You sure about that? Because pushing you straight off a cliff sounds pretty damn appealing right about now."

His eyes narrowed, challenge banked in their depths. "Try me. Now you either come out of this damn cabin on your own two feet, or so help me, River, I will toss you over my shoulder and carry you, in that goddamned towel, ass hanging out, pussy on display for the entire fucking ranch to see."

A little shiver of heat curled in my belly. I wanted nothing to do with that caveman display, but I'd be lying to myself if I tried to deny the way my body reacted to it.

"You touch me with any part of you, be prepared for me to bite it off, Cross."

"That a promise?"

"It's a goddamn fact."

"At least I'd get those pretty lips of yours wrapped around me one last time."

Walker watched all of this with a hangdog expression. "Let her be," he said, voice low and tight.

I shot him a withering look. "Don't help me."

He lifted his hands in a gesture of surrender, and I stomped past him into the bedroom, slamming the door on both of them while I pulled on my clothes from the day before. If that arrogant ass thought I was going anywhere near him or his horse, he didn't have a damn brain in his head.

I peeked out the window and saw his saddled horse tied to the hitching post, and a wicked grin curled my lips.

But I sure as hell would steal Hades and leave him here to

find his own way back. The thought of Cross riding behind Walker, with his arms wrapped around his waist, had me chuckling to myself.

Would serve them right.

I made my way to the window, pushing it open as silently as possible before climbing out.

"Going somewhere?"

Sterling's soft rumble made me tense before the amused curl of his lips told me he wasn't here to stop me. The man was leaning against the tree outside my window, his irises bright silver and filled with mirth as he took me in.

"That depends. Whose side are you on?"

"The boss's."

Lifting my chin, I forced myself to exude confidence I didn't really feel right now. "That's me. Take me back to the lodge? I've had about enough of the Cross brothers."

"Whatever you need."

I hadn't realized how badly I needed an ally—no, a friend—until that moment. "You're a good man, Sterling Bishop."

His eyes turned stormy. "No, siren. I'm not."

Despite his protest, I didn't believe him. Only a good man would try to convince you he was bad. It was the bad ones who pretended to be good. Case in point, the Cross brothers. No, Sterling was more like Bear. A good man who did bad things. I could live with that. At least he was honest about it.

I always had a thing for Robin Hood. Now I understood why.

"You riding with me, or are we stealing his horse?"

"Would you be comfortable having me ride with you? I thought about horse theft, but honestly, I don't want to see Cross again for as long as I live, and if I steal Hades, there's no way he'll leave me alone."

That flicker of indecision in his eyes told me he'd struggle with our proximity, but then he gave a curt nod.

"You sit in front, keep your hands on the horn. I'll do the rest."

I couldn't resist flirting a bit as I fell into position beside him. "So is this how it is with you?"

"How what is?"

"You doing all the work?"

He swallowed, silent for a beat before he answered. "I like to be in control. I need it."

A little shiver ran down my spine at the darkness in his tone. Bishop was so different from the others, and right now, I was damn glad he was here. I was still furious with Cross and Walker, but the fire they'd lit inside me was fading with every second I spent in my giant's presence. There was just something about him. Something that made me feel like he wouldn't let anything hurt me, not even himself.

Maybe the best way to get over a cowboy was to get under another one.

"You need help mounting?" he asked as we approached his horse.

I shook my head, knowing it would be hard for him to put his hands on me, and this ride was already going to cause him discomfort.

"I've got it."

I mounted smoothly from the ground, even though the animal was a very large workhorse. These long legs of mine came in handy every once in a while. I fought the urge to grimace as my bruises reminded me they were still there and protested the position, but I needed to get back, and this was the only way unless I wanted to walk.

Bishop joined me, sitting behind the saddle, hands taking the reins while mine rested on the horn, exactly as he'd told me.

He leaned close, lips at my ear as he whispered, "You're fucking perfect just like that. Don't move."

I should not have been so turned on by his words while

Walker's cum was still inside me, but fuck if my pussy got the memo.

"I said don't. The way you're squirming isn't making this any easier."

I hadn't even realized I was moving. But by the way his bulge pressed into my ass, I'd say this was definitely making things harder.

"I hate to break it to you, but the second we take off, I'm going to be moving whether you like it or not."

Moving . . . and bouncing . . . and rubbing . . .

He grunted behind me, his breath fanning over the back of my shoulders.

"I'll survive."

With a gentle command, he set the horse walking away from the cabin, his hips rolling into mine.

We'd only just crested the hill when Cross and Walker ran out of the cabin.

"Get back here, River!"

I gave Cross a single-finger salute and a sassy grin.

"Can this thing go any faster? I really don't want them to catch us."

Bishop's chuckle vibrated through my back. "Hold on tight. Ghost can really fly."

seventeen

Bishop

"So, Walker, huh?" I asked after putting Ghost away.

River was fiddling with a length of rope hanging from a hook nearby, her slender fingers sliding over the fibers, making me picture her with a very different kind of rope. One that made it impossible for her to put her hands on me but gave me access to every inch of her.

Having her touching me so close and for so long, her warm body constantly brushing mine, had been almost too much to bear on our ride back, but I'd survived.

"Nope."

The way she popped the P told me she really didn't want to talk about it. Unfortunately, I wasn't going to give her the luxury of hiding. The information was too damn useful.

"That's not what it looked like." Or sounded like, for that matter. With the way the three of them had been carrying on, I doubted a person on this ranch didn't know what went down in that cabin last night.

"Looks can be deceiving. Just like Walker fucking Cross."

Okay, then. I shrugged. "His loss."

She scoffed. "Yeah. You could say that." Her gaze didn't meet mine as she continued trailing her hand across the coiled lasso. "Could've done without the lies, though. I'm not a fan of snakes."

"Need me to have a talk with him?" All my protective instincts flared to life at the defensiveness in her voice and the defeated slump of her shoulders. He'd really hurt her.

"You gonna defend my honor, Sterling?"

"Does it need defending, siren?"

That earned me her deep green irises. "I hate to break it to you, cowboy, but you're about ten years too late to rescue me from the Cross boys."

"I'm not a cowboy. Not really."

"You wanna tell that to those spurs you're wearing?"

"That's a matter of practicality. Never hurts to have the right tools for the job."

"Uh huh." Her teasing smirk lit a fire in my belly. "Would you rather I call you 'soldier' instead?"

"I already told you, call me Sterling."

She straightened and closed the distance between us, not coming within touching distance, but still putting all her attention on me. "Thanks for getting me out of there, Sterling. I was this close to castrating one or both of them."

I couldn't tell if she was serious, and I didn't want to find out.

"So why stick around, then?" I didn't realize how much I wanted to know the answer until the question left my lips. A foolish part of me wanted it to be because she wanted to spend more time with me, which was stupid for any number of reasons.

"I already told you about the will."

I studied her long and hard. "Nah, I'm not buying it. That gives you an excuse, but it's not the real reason. Woman like you . . . you'd find a way around it if you really needed to."

"It seemed pretty ironclad to me," she said, but her eyes darted to the side, and it was all the proof I needed that I'd just hit the nail on the head.

"Siren, what aren't you saying?"

"I have my reasons." The way she stiffened then turned away from me only added to my unease. There was a whole hell of a lot more going on than she wanted to admit.

I TOOK her chin between my fingers and tipped her face back to mine, a little jolt of electricity shooting through me at the contact. I released her just as quickly, but she didn't look away.

"If you tell me, I might be able to help you."

She opened and closed her mouth several times, looking torn, before releasing a heavy breath. "Someone's sending me letters."

I don't know what the fuck I thought she might say, but that sure as shit wasn't it.

"What kind of fucking letters? Is someone threatening you?" The hairs on the back of my neck stood on end.

"No. Maybe?" She bit down on her lip, and I had the sudden instinct to tug it free.

"Well, which is it?"

"I'm not sure. They're about my parents."

"Show me."

Indecision flitted through her eyes, but the moment I reached out and cupped her nape, crossing the touch barrier once more, she caved.

"They're in my room."

"Let's go."

I dropped my hand as soon as she started walking, but instead of the relief I'd usually feel, there was a pang of regret. Everything about this woman twisted me up inside. There wasn't a single person I could think of I willingly initiated touch with. In the rare instances I'd given in and sought out a partner to sate my lust, they'd always followed a strict set of rules.

No emotion.

No repeats.

No fucking touching.

My dick sliding through their pussy didn't count, but even then, I controlled when and how. Since returning to civilian life, those encounters had been few and far between, though, because the risk of triggering my PTSD was too high. One wrong move from them could be deadly. After a near miss, I chose a life of celibacy in order to protect myself and others. Wasn't like I could have a real relationship anyway, and sex wasn't worth it if I couldn't trust my own hands. I did just fine on my own.

"Come on in," River said when we arrived at her bedroom door.

I followed her, the subtle floral scent of her fragrance hitting my nose as I did.

"How many letters have you received so far?" I asked, more as a way to bring my mind back to the possible danger she was in and not on the fact that there was a bed nearby and I was dying to know what she tasted like when she came.

"Just the two. Hang on." She strode over to the bed, bent over—fuck me, she had the perfect ass—and pulled two manila envelopes from between the mattress and box spring.

"That's not a very safe place to be hiding things you don't want found," I scolded.

"Under the mattresses. Isn't that a thing? Like from The Godfather?"

I chuckled. "No, that's 'to the mattresses.' Not the same thing. It means go to war."

"Well, as long as Ghost's head doesn't end up on my pillow . . ."

I gaped at her. "Why would I ever do that?"

"Because of that one scene, you know? With the horse head and the bloody sheets. I dunno . . . I was just saying."

"You leave Ghost out of it, you pretty little psychopath."

She laughed. "And you say you aren't a real cowboy."

"I'm not."

"The way you love that horse says different."

Pressing my lips together to keep from smiling, I reached out and snatched the letters from her. One was still sealed.

"You haven't opened it?"

A soft flush stole across her cheeks. "I'm sort of afraid to. The first was bad enough. I could hardly sleep for a few nights after. The pictures were . . . a lot."

Sliding the pictures out of the letter in question, I stared down at a grisly crime scene. "Jesus." I set the stack face down once I'd finished, glancing over at her before I opened the second. "Do you mind?"

"No, please. I'd rather you do it than me."

I gave her a sharp nod and slid my finger beneath the edge, opening the envelope and allowing the new stack of pictures to slide out. These were worse than the first.

In those, the couple had been shot execution-style, making it seem like that had been the extent of it. But these pictures told a different story. One that said being shot had been a mercy compared to the agony they'd experienced. It also proved that their bodies had been staged in the last set, made to look like the gunshots were the worst of their injuries. Sadly, that was just the tip of the iceberg.

In this new set of photos, the couple was naked, chained up, and very much alive. Given the state of their bodies, that was not necessarily a good thing. They'd been beaten, for days, if I had to guess. Tortured without a doubt, given the number of cigarette burns and cuts marring their skin. But it was the word carved into each of their chests that made my stomach curdle.

Traitor.

What was worse, though, were the very clear burn marks next to those words. The Twisted Cross Ranch brand stood out like a beacon, the intertwined TCR recognizable to anyone in this town. Shit. I couldn't let her see this. Not if I was any kind of man.

"What is it?" she asked, voice quavering.

I shook my head. "I think it might be best if you don't ask me questions you don't really want the answers to, siren." I'd hand them over if she demanded it; they were hers by right. But I couldn't in good conscience show them to her without preparing her for the reality they contained. She didn't need those kinds of nightmares, not when I could spare her.

River gulped. "That bad, huh?"

My jaw tightened as I nodded. "Worse."

The subtle flare of her eyes told me she knew it had to be if I was the one saying so. I'd told her enough about my background for her to guess at the sorts of horrors I'd seen. I wouldn't tell her it was bad if it wasn't fucking awful.

"Fuck." She didn't stop me when I slid the pictures back into the envelope. "Tell me what I need to know."

"The murders were linked to Twisted Cross Ranch, and they weren't killed on the road."

"But the crime scene . . ."

"Was staged. Someone took them first, and when they were done playing with them, they used their bodies to send a message."

"W-why?"

"I don't know. But I'm going to help you find out."

"How?"

"I still have some contacts in the service who owe me favors." It was the truth, even if it was misleading.

Her face paled as she sank onto the bed. "Who would hurt them? They were good, kind people. I don't understand any of this. Why send these to me after all these years? How are the Crosses involved?" She swallowed and dropped her head in her hands.

I reached for her, but pulled my shaking hand back before she saw me. My own monsters were too close to the surface right now. The anxiety buzzing through my veins had me nearly gasping for breath as the past threatened to infiltrate my mind.

"I'll make some calls. See what I can do. Stay here. Lock your door. I'll come for you in the morning."

"You think I'm in danger?" Her big eyes swam with unshed tears as she lifted her head and stared up at me.

Knowing what I did about the Cross family, there was no way I could say no without it being a lie. And the last thing I wanted to do was lie to her—more than I already was.

"Just stay here until I come for you." I leveled my gaze on her. "Promise me."

"Promise."

With one last look, I turned and walked out of her room, waiting until I heard the soft click of the lock before I pulled my phone out and dialed a number from memory.

My contact answered on the first ring, his rough, gravelly rumble doing nothing to hide his annoyance. "It's about damn time you checked in. The brass is crawling up my ass looking for a status report."

"This goes deeper than we thought."

There was a long pause before he responded. "Is this line secure?"

"Not secure enough for what I have to tell you."

"Usual spot, thirteen hundred hours?"

"I'll be there."

eighteen

River

I surged out of the water, still warm despite the late hour. Or early, I supposed, depending on your way of thinking. The drama of the last few weeks was catching up with me. Between avoiding the Cross brothers and waiting for Bishop to hear back from his contact about my parents, I was constantly on edge and barely sleeping. It had been two days since I'd shown Bishop the pictures and beside his assurances, we weren't any closer to finding out who was behind the notes. Which is why I was swimming laps at two in the morning, trying to exhaust myself enough to force the issue.

Except I'd gone thirty laps, and even as I sat on the pool's edge, breaths heaving, skin buzzing, muscles trembling, my mind still swirled as much as it had been before.

"Goddamn you, Walker. You ruined everything," I whispered to myself as I got to my feet and toweled off before pulling on a cover-up.

I half expected the handsome dick to saunter out of the shadows and try to win me over with his charming grin and a few 'darlin's.' He didn't. The grounds were eerily quiet, the wind in the trees and the occasional bray of the cattle in the distance the soundtrack of the night.

"Fuck it," I grumbled, stomping my way back into the house. Instead of making the turn that would lead me to the guest room I'd claimed, I went the other direction toward Senior's office. I didn't much feel like staring at the ceiling until the sun came up. Might as well make use of my insomnia and get some work done.

I'd been going through the business reports, making my own observations and lists about which businesses were "clean" versus "dirty" and trying to reconcile that with what I'd already found in the second set of books hidden in Senior's desk. Spoiler alert, not many were clean. This family had more skeletons in their closet than a damn cemetery.

Leaving the lights off in the office, I strode toward the desk, intent on continuing to build my case against them. I needed some insurance in case I was implicated in anything now that I was majority owner. I knew better than to assume that the Crosses didn't have dirty politicians on their side. Being innocent wouldn't be enough to keep my ass out of trouble if they were going to use me as a scapegoat. I needed proof. A lot of it. Thus my lists. They had their secrets. I would have mine.

Whatever happened, I wouldn't go down with them. But a part of me knew if anything came out about them, my family legacy might also be tarnished. My dad had been involved, if the books were any indication.

A little shudder traversed my spine. I hadn't opened that envelope since Bishop warned me against it. I wasn't usually one to bury my head in the sand, but those were my parents in the pictures, and I'd seen the look of disgust cross his face when he'd flipped through the stack. Anything that could make a man like him look like *that* didn't need to ruin my memories of them. What I'd found in the first set was bad enough.

I turned on the small desk lamp as I sat in the oversized chair, my thoughts still racing, fatigue a distant memory. But something unusual caught my eye in my periphery. A soft glow coming from the ostentatious wood-burning fireplace on the left wall. This wasn't embers or a gas pilot light. It was a line of cool light, starting from the floor and going about chest height, coming from the back corner. As if the entire back wall of the fireplace had shifted.

Without a second thought, I stood and approached the hearth. A stream of cold air filtered out of the crack, and as I pushed on the bricks, the wall rotated open. It was a false back—no, it was a goddamn secret passage.

"Jesus, if Mr. Boddy is waiting for me in the library with a candlestick, I'm getting the fuck out of here."

I had to admit, I was a little sad no one was around to appreciate my excellent *Clue* reference.

Glancing inside, I frowned at the dimly lit hole with nothing more than a ladder and a breeze to greet me. I'd be an idiot to climb down there. Wouldn't I?

Unfortunately my curiosity outweighed any sense of self-preservation I had. I needed to know where this passage led. Especially if it might help me answer questions about the business I'd inherited. Or even more importantly, help me avenge my parent's murders. And since I didn't exactly know how the passage opened, this might be my only opportunity.

I couldn't waste it.

Taking a steadying breath, I began a slow, careful climb down, thankful for the light provided by the lone bare bulb mounted at the bottom. At least I wasn't lowering myself into a pit of blackness. A concrete tunnel greeted me once my feet hit the ground, void of anything save those sporadic light-bulbs that flickered ominously as far as the eye could see. It smelled of damp and disuse down here, but I also noted the occasional rust-colored stain on the walls here and there. Blood? Or actual rust? I was hoping for the latter.

There was no way to know for sure how long I walked. It had to be at least ten minutes, but I'd long stopped counting Mississippis, so it could have been more or less.

A chill broke out across my skin—being underground and in nothing but a wet swimsuit and terry cloth cover-up wasn't the best choice for this kind of exploring. Just when I thought I'd never reach the end of this corridor, a doorway appeared about twenty feet from me. I'd expected to find another ladder, but this was a partially open metal door, light spilling through the crack.

But that wasn't all. There were also voices. Specifically two voices. One an angry growl I'd recognize anywhere. The other reduced to pitiful screams.

My stomach rolled, and I was no longer confident in my quest for answers, but I'd come this far. I had to see it through.

Creeping closer, I peered inside and had to fight the urge to gasp as Cross loomed over the naked, bleeding man he'd tied to a chair. His fist connected with the guy's cheek, bloody spittle flying as he made contact.

"Who hired you?" Cross snarled, grabbing a hammer and raising it.

From this vantage point, I could see the restrained man, his chair positioned so he was facing me. They must have been at this for a while if the amount of blood dripping down the guy was any indication. The only obstruction preventing me from seeing the full extent of the damage was Cross. His broad shoulders and muscular back partially blocked my view.

My former lover was dressed down—for him—in just a T-shirt and jeans. But that's not what my eyes focused on. They were trained on the gun tucked into his waistband.

"Don't make me ask you again!"

The man grunted, then spat in Cross's face, the tattoo on his neck bulging as he put force behind the gesture.

This was the man who stabbed Walker. There was no doubt in my mind. That angel tattoo was as distinctive as it got.

"You hurt my brother. That means you tried to hurt me. Now tell me who fucking put out the hit on him, and maybe I'll show you some mercy."

"He'll kill me if he finds out."

"I'm going to kill you if you don't."

"You're gonna kill me anyway."

"So what do you have to lose?"

"Besides my dignity?"

Cross's head dipped to the obvious puddle beneath the man. "I think we're long past that."

"I . . . I'm . . ." the man heaved for breath, struggling. Cross stood there, waiting, hammer in hand. "I'm sorry . . ." He coughed. "I'm sorry I didn't kill him like Dominik wanted."

My body trembled as I anticipated what was coming next.

"Thank you for your candor." Cross pulled his gun from the back of his pants, cocked it, and took aim.

I couldn't watch. I turned on my heel and bolted in the only direction I could. Back the way I came. The shot rang out, so loud it made my ears hurt as the sound bounced off the tunnel walls, seeming to stretch on forever. I yelped on reflex, and all I could do was hope Cross hadn't heard me.

nineteen

. . .

Cross

I heard the little yip of fear as the echo of the gunshot bounced off the walls. What the fuck was that? No one should be down here. Hell, no one knew about this place except Walker, and he was passed the fuck out after yet another night of drowning his sorrows over River.

A low growl of frustration escaped as I realized I was going to have to check the noise out and leave clean up for later. Wasn't like this asshole was going anywhere.

Frantic footsteps reverberated through the underground passage. The sound, mixed with soft, feminine whimpers, pulled me out of the room. There was only one woman on this property, and she didn't belong down here.

Shoving open the door, I caught the flash of her hair and knew I needed to run damage control. What was she doing up? It was nearly three a.m., for God's sake.

"River?"

She let out another soft cry and picked up her pace.

"Goddammit." The words were bitten off, but they bounced down the corridor as if I'd shouted them, tucking my gun back into my jeans as I took off after her.

"Stay away from me, Cross."

I should let her run. I'd wanted her to stay out of my way, but I hated the idea of her being afraid of me. After what she'd just witnessed, how could she be anything but? I didn't just shoot that guy. I'd tortured him. Who knows how much of that she'd seen? I had to find out. I had to make sure she kept her fucking mouth shut.

Maybe it was best she was scared, after all.

If she was afraid of us, she'd stop digging. She'd get the hell out of here and leave us be.

If she leaves, that bastard could buy us out at public auction . . .

River Adams was a liability no matter where she went. But which was worse? Her getting caught up in my family's business, or her being the reason we lost it all?

"Stay away?" I spat, closing in on her as she continued her mad dash to the exit.

I didn't need to let her in on the fact that the other end of this tunnel opened up under the stables. She wouldn't get past me anyway.

I snagged her by the elbow, spinning her to face me and halting her progress.

I'd expected fear but ended up facing fury. If looks could kill, I'd be nothing but a husk. She was a constant surprise. Chest heaving, eyes bright with emotion, she didn't cower but held my gaze. Christ, she was beautiful. I'd almost forgotten what the two of us were doing when her words brought me back.

"I saw what you were doing to that man. You . . . he's dead, isn't he?"

He was, and I'd do it again in a heartbeat if it meant keeping my brother safe. *Her* safe. She could have so easily been collateral damage that night. She didn't have a fucking clue about the devils breathing down her neck. About the danger her connection to us put her in.

I intended to keep it that way.

Clenching my jaw, I forced in a long, slow breath and tried

to ignore the little voice in the back of my head telling me to kiss her. To claim her.

"You don't need to know any more than you already do, sparrow."

"Don't pretend like you're trying to protect me. You're scared."

I scoffed. "Scared of what? You? Unlikely."

"Scared of what I can do to you. I have your balls in my hand, and all I have to do is cut them off with a flick of my wrist, Danny. I could walk away and let this place burn."

That was the last thing I could let her do.

I tugged her closer, my voice dropping to a furious whisper. "You don't know a fuckin' thing."

"I know enough. More than enough to go to the police."

"That's an empty threat, and you know it."

"Wanna try me, Cross?"

The challenge in her was like a careful dance between us. She moved, I moved. We were playing a game, and I was never quite sure of the rules. I'd be lying if I said I didn't get a thrill out of it. With her, fighting felt a helluva lot like foreplay.

"I don't have to. We both know anything you say to the cops will ruin you as much as us. Don't you get it, sweetheart? You *are* Twisted Cross Ranch now. Senior saw to that. You wanna take us down? You'll topple right down beside us."

Her unease wasn't as strong as I'd hoped. I wanted fear to flash through those green irises. I needed it, because then I'd trust she would act to protect herself, if not us. Truth was, she'd left us all behind with no love lost, and she'd probably be happy to watch us burn, even at the cost of her reputation. We certainly hadn't given her a reason to want anything else. But maybe there was one more card I could play. Because she might hate the Cross men, but she loved her parents, and the Adamses' legacy was tied to ours. Even in death.

It may have been ten years ago, but I'd heard her thin voice on the phone when she'd called to check in after she couldn't reach them. That awful day when I'd stood next to my father as he told her they were dead and that she couldn't come back for the funeral.

She wasn't the kind of girl to get over that crushing grief. I bet it controlled her still. In fact, I was counting on it.

"It'll ruin your precious daddy's reputation."

She sucked in a sharp breath, her eyes widening.

Bingo.

"That's right, sparrow. Your daddy's hands were just as dirty as ours."

"I hate you."

"The feeling's mutual. Now climb your ass up the ladder and get out of my hair. If you know what's good for you, you'll go to bed and forget this tunnel even exists. You hear me? Unless you want to help me clean up my mess. Or should I say, our mess?"

"You're a monster." Her voice was low and controlled, fury burning behind the words.

"Yeah, well, you're the one who spread her legs for me. What does that make you?"

Her palm was a blur of motion as she slapped me across the cheek. I'd earned that one. Hell, I wouldn't put it past her to smother me in my sleep at this point, but if we stayed enemies, I didn't have to ever lose her. Wasn't that how it worked? You couldn't lose what you never had in the first place.

But you did have her.

Once.

I rolled my head from side to side, letting the sting of her strike radiate through me. Oddly, it hurt less than my memories. If anything, her hand on me only fueled my desire for her. Fucked up, I know, but I was hardly going to judge myself for having an honest reaction. I was a violent man; it was only natural.

"Feel better?"

"No." She slapped me again.

"You about done?"

"Fighting you? Never."

Her fire had me hard as stone, and I hated how I reacted to her. Not just physically. Emotionally. She had me tied up in knots, and I didn't have fucking time for this. I had a dead Russian in my storeroom, a still unresolved hit on my brother, and a shipment going out soon I was certain would be sabotaged. My empire was literally falling apart, and she stood at the center of it all.

"So what you're telling me is I should haul your ass up that ladder. Because the only way you're getting out of here is with me right behind you."

"You just want to look at my ass."

"I don't need you on a ladder to do that. Now go."

She followed my instructions without arguing for once, and I'm not ashamed to admit I did stare as she climbed. For a second, I worried she'd try to close me in before I could get up and into the office, but she didn't. She was waiting for me, leaning up against the desk.

"Happy?" she asked.

"Not remotely."

"Any other secret kill rooms hiding under the house?"

"If there are, I'm sure as fuck not telling you."

"I'll just get the blueprint from McCreedy."

"Who says we put the *secret* rooms on the blueprints?"

She narrowed her eyes at me. "One way or another, I'll uncover all your dirty laundry, Cross."

"I'm sure you'll try. But remember, yours is just as dirty now."

"We'll see about that."

"What the hell is that supposed to mean?" I shouted after her as she turned and stormed out of the office.

It took everything in me not to chase after her and demand she answer me. But I was in no shape to traipse through the house. As it was, I'd just earned myself extra cleaning time making sure that asshole's blood hadn't found its way into my father's office. Fuck, she riled me up like no one else could. She made me sloppy. I couldn't afford that. I needed to keep my head in the game, not lost in her.

So, with a heavy sigh, I pulled out my phone and made a call.

As soon as the call connected, I simply said, "I need a deep clean. ASAP."

twenty

. . .

River

I couldn't stop myself from flicking my attention to the huge fireplace as I sat at the desk in the office and worked on reconciling financials. Try as I might, Cross's parting shot from last night ran through my mind.

"...yours is just as dirty now."

The pencil I'd been using to tally up numbers snapped as I ground my teeth together. I wasn't sure who I was angrier at, Cross or myself.

I'd let him get to me. Again.

Daniel Cross knew exactly where to poke me to make me react. I hated him but still wanted to see him. Part of me said that was only because he was a cold-blooded killer, and I needed to know where he was in case he decided to take out the only witness to his heinous crime. The other, much more thirsty part just wanted to look at him. I was a damn mess.

He's a fucking murderer, River. Get it together. We do not lust after murderers.

My brain needed to have a chat with my vagina because my panties were telling a different story.

"Focus. Math takes focus," I muttered, but it was no use. I was one big ball of distraction.

Not that anyone could blame me. The events of the last couple of weeks were straight out of a soap opera. Normal life was not supposed to be like this, filled with stabbings, secret passageways, and torture rooms—not to mention three gorgeous men with questionable morals. But then, my life hadn't been normal in a long time.

"Ugh, this is useless." Throwing my hands in the air, I stared up at the ornate design on the tin ceiling tiles and began counting the repeated fleur-de-lis patterns.

The familiar ding I recognized as an email arriving came from Senior's computer, dragging my gaze down.

"Think of it as *our* email now, Senior," I said under my breath as his portrait stared me down across the room. I kept meaning to take that ostentatious piece of garbage down. The eyes seemed to follow me around the room. But I'd sort of gotten used to venting my frustration at it, and along the way it grew on me. Maybe I could turn it into a dartboard or something?

I clicked on the email and read aloud as I toyed with the remains of the pencil I'd mutilated.

"Reminder, you are invited to the annual Cattleman's Gala this Saturday night at 7:00 p.m. Sponsored by Fairbanks Meats and Cross Industries."

A fucking gala? Why hadn't anyone told me about this?

Further down the email, I spotted a personalized note.

To: CEO@crossindustries.com
From: C.Davenport@Cattlemansociety.org
Subject: Reminder: Cattleman's Gala

Dear Mr. Cross,

Reminder, you are invited to the annual Cattleman's Gala and silent auction this Saturday night at 7:00 p.m. Sponsored by Fairbanks Meats and Cross Industries.

We still haven't received your RSVP and would love to know if we can expect you or a representative of the Cross family to accept the posthumous lifetime achievement award we'll be presenting in your father's honor.

Sincerely,
Cecilia Davenport
Secretary to Milo Quinn, Chairman of the Cattleman Society

PS I personally would love to see you again. It's been far too long since you pushed me around on the dance floor. Xoxo, Cici

"CICI? Who the fuck is Cici? This bitch can take her hugs and kisses somewhere else. Like right up her damn ass." I frowned and read through the email again. "I would personally love to see you again," I mocked. "It's been far too long since you shoved that mighty big dick of yours in my juicy fuckhole . . ."

Petty? Absolutely.

Did I remotely care? Nope. Not one bit.

Fuck her and the Cross she rode in on.

Only one woman was getting screwed by this family, and right now, it was me. Metaphorically, of course. We were done with the literal screwing.

I dropped my head in my hands, annoyed at the mere thought of having to watch either brother flirt with someone right in front of me. I could only imagine how well it would go down if I tried to do the same.

Wait a damn second.

Why couldn't I?

My new gal pal Cici had just given me the perfect opportunity to get a little revenge of my own. Returning my attention to the computer, I shook out my hands and gleefully sent my reply to old Cici.

To: C.Davenport@Cattlemansociety.org
From: CEO@crossindustries.com
Subject: re: Reminder: Cattleman's Gala

My dear Cici,

I would be delighted to see you again. You can count on us attending. Please send over four tickets at your earliest convenience. Also, if it's not too late, I'd love to donate a month's worth of personally instructed horseback riding lessons to the silent auction.

X

I HIT SEND BEFORE GIVING myself a chance to chicken out. Cross was going to lose his ever-loving mind when he found out I'd just volunteered him for one-on-one time with some snot-nosed kid.

Now I just needed a date. And I had the perfect burly bear of a man in mind.

In a perfect world, I'd just ask Bishop. I would love to see him all dressed up and waltz around on his arm, but an event like that would be his version of hell, and if I asked, he'd feel compelled to say yes. I couldn't do that to the man who'd stepped up as my protector. And even if crowds and proximity weren't triggers for him, his loyalty was to more than just me. He was entrenched in Twisted Cross Ranch, and that meant there were at least some tethers to the Cross family. I needed someone I knew. Someone I had history with and trusted beyond all doubt.

I didn't just need a date. I needed a confidant.

Pulling out my phone, I dialed Bear's number and waited to see if he'd answer. There was no telling with the man. If he'd been up late working for the club, he'd still be dead to the world this early, but there were mornings he'd met me at my door for sunrise walks too. He was unpredictable about everything—except his devotion to the people in his life.

"What's wrong, cub?" His deep, growly voice was thick with sleep. So it had been a late night then.

"You said you'd come if I needed you. That offer still good?"

"Yeah. Just say the word." The rustle of fabric in the background, followed by a woman's soft, unmistakable sigh, made me feel even more guilty for disturbing him.

"There's been some shit going down out here. I don't have any allies. Don't know who to trust."

"Have they hurt you?"

Not unless you count my pride.

"No. Nothing like that."

Internally my brain was screaming, *not yet*. There was no telling what Cross would do to me if I got in his way. We might have history, but he'd proven how little that meant.

"I've been doing some digging. Unearthing a lot of dark shit. I don't know who I can talk to, but you . . . you're not part of this."

"Okay, look, I've got some loose ends to tie up. I can be there in a week or so. Is that soon enough, or do you need me to catch a flight out today?"

I sighed. "Next week is fine. It doesn't give me a date for

this event I have to attend, but it does ease my mind knowing you'll be here to help me deal."

"You sure, cub?"

"Yeah, I'm sure. Thanks, Bear."

"All right. See you soon."

"See ya." I started to hang up, but his voice had me pull the phone back in time to catch the rest of what he was saying.

"Give 'em hell."

"Oh, I intend to."

"That's my girl."

I hung up feeling loads better than I had before our chat. That solved one of my problems, but not the more immediate issue of needing a plus one for this gala.

"Well, Bishop, it looks like I'll have to ask you to be my plus one after all," I muttered, spotting him out the window to my right.

"Plus one to what, darlin'?" Walker's voice made me flinch, the sexy drawl hitting me straight in the gut.

"None of your business." I closed the laptop and stood, but Walker rounded on me, lifting open the computer and smirking when the screen went right back to the open email.

"Oh, shit. Cross is gonna have a hissy fit when he finds out."

"Won't that be fun. If you'll excuse me, I need to go shopping for a dress to wear to this event y'all didn't see fit to tell me about."

He snagged my wrist as I tried to walk away from him, the heat of his skin on mine reminding me of the way his touch branded me that night in the cabin.

"Don't be that way, ladybug. I'm . . . I hate thinkin' you're mad at me."

I jerked my arm away from him. "I am mad at you, Walker. I'm so mad I could spit. You used me."

"No, I didn't."

"Don't lie. Don't be like your brother. I heard everything you said. I am not here to be toyed with or *distracted*. I refuse to be a pawn in whatever sick game the two of you are playing. You may have been my best friend once, Walker Cross, but you are nothing to me now."

twenty-one

. . .

Walker

River knew exactly where to hit me and make it hurt. But then again, she had a right to be upset. She didn't know the truth, that I was head over fucking heels for her and 'distracting' her had been an excuse for me to get close to her without Cross butting in. Just because my brother thought I'd been going along with his plan didn't make it true. But she hadn't heard any of that. She was operating with only a part of the story, admittedly the worst part, but if I could get her to listen to me, she'd realize she had me pegged all wrong.

"Don't say things you don't mean, darlin'. We have something special between us. You and I both know it."

"Had. We *had* something special. Until you turned out to be a lying, manipulative asshole, just like Cross."

"I never lied to you. Nothing about what we did together was a lie."

She cocked a brow. "So you weren't trying to distract me with that magic dick of yours?"

My lips twitched before I could help it. "I mean, you're the one calling it magic." She was thoroughly unamused, so I cleared my throat. "And no, I wasn't trying to distract you." If possible, her brow rose even higher. "Okay, yes, Cross told me to, but that's not what this was. Is. Fuck." I blew out a frustrated breath. "I'm not saying this right."

"You're not saying much of anything. All I hear is that you don't even know why you did it. I don't have casual sex, Walker. I was in a place where I was vulnerable, and I shared that with you. I told you about my confusing feelings for all three of you, and you were there for me. But it turned ugly the moment the truth came out. You can't just backpedal and gaslight me."

"I'm not—" I let out a frustrated groan and raked my fingers through my hair. "Would you just listen to me, woman? I'm trying to tell you how I feel about you, and all you can see fit to do is yell at me."

"Oh, I'm sorry. Are your feelings hurt? Do you need a fucking cookie? You used me. You used my feelings for you against me, all as part of some scheme your brother cooked up to keep my nose out of your business. Well, joke's on you. It didn't fucking work."

"Goddammit, River. I didn't use you. I've been in love with you since we were kids. I was finally getting everything I wanted. You finally saw *me* instead of him. You wanted me. So, dammit, I took the opportunity and made you mine. Not his. Even if he hadn't asked me to distract you, I would've been there by your side. I'd do anything for you. Always have and always will."

Her eyes flared, and I could tell I'd surprised her, but she was quick to school her expression. "Excuse me if I have a little trouble believing that. It's not like I heard from you once while I was gone, Walker. Your actions are speaking a whole helluva lot louder than your words."

"If you think I didn't try to find you, you're dead wrong. But every time, they put a stop to it. Cross and my dad, I mean. They said to leave you be. That you'd be safer wherever you were. That I was no good for you and the best thing we could do for you was let you hide."

"My parents died, Walker!" she shouted, standing up and stalking over to poke me in the chest. "You think I didn't need my best friend?"

"They told me you were next!" I shouted back. "What the hell was I supposed to do? If people were watching me, which I can only assume they were, given how close we were, I couldn't lead them back to you. I had to let you go." My voice cracked, and I couldn't think straight around the emotions crowding my head. "They always say if you love something, let it go, and if it's really yours, it will come back. Well, it took ten fucking years, but you came back. You're mine, darlin'. I won't ever let you go again."

"All this time?" she asked softly.

I moved closer, hands itching to reach for her and pull her into my chest, but when I did, she jerked away.

"You knew?"

That was it? That was all she was gonna say after I bled out all over the damn floor. "That I loved you? Of course I fucking knew."

Suspicion burned in her eyes. "No, Walker. You knew my parents were murdered?"

Shit.

Any ground I'd won was immediately lost as those verdant eyes of hers shuttered. There was no digging myself out of this hole.

"Go away, Walker."

"No, not until we settle this."

My phone chose that exact moment to start ringing. I pulled it out of my pocket to silence it, but not before River got a look at the caller's name. Cross.

"Oh look, your handler's calling. Better answer it before he takes away your allowance."

I ignored his call and focused on the woman in front of

me. She was slipping through my fingers, and if I didn't at least salvage some of this relationship, I'd never be able to win her back.

"I don't care about what he has to say. I'm not giving up on fixing this between us."

"What part of there is no us are you having trouble understanding?"

"All of it. Because it's bullshit, and you know it."

River shook her head at me. "You're as stubborn as your brother."

"Runs in our blood."

"Just . . ." My girl sighed, some of the fight leaving her as she looked away from me. "Just leave me alone, Walker. I've got a stupid gala to prepare for."

This was my chance. "Let me take you. I'll be your date."

Apprehension flashed in her eyes. "It's not that easy, Walker. You can't just say some pretty words and expect me to fall into your arms and be okay with everything that happened. I'm not going to the gala with you. You're not my knight in shining armor or the handsome prince sweeping me off my feet. You're the rake who ruins the heroine. Not the hero."

"So what you're telling me is I need to make a grand gesture."

"That is literally not anywhere close to what I just said."

I flashed her my most charming grin. "Don't worry, darlin', I heard you loud and clear."

"Did you? I don't think you did."

My phone rang again, Cross's name appearing like a countdown to doomsday. If I didn't answer him this time, he'd come hauling ass down the hall and tear me a new one.

"You should get that," she murmured, turning away, but I caught her wrist.

"We're not finished with this, ladybug. I don't use the word love lightly. I intend to prove it to you."

This time I didn't give her a chance to refute my words or throw them back in my face. I gave her a quick peck on the lips she was too surprised to stop and then walked out of the office, answering my phone as I did.

"What?"

"We've got a big fucking problem."

THIRTY MINUTES LATER, I was with my brother in what I'd affectionately dubbed the 'wet room.' It was the hidden storage room beneath the stables where all manner of sins occurred, most notably those of the bloody variety. It was also the only place the two of us could talk without being overheard. River's ears had always been pressed to the walls when we were kids. The last thing she needed to hear was this.

"The shipments that didn't make weigh-in were from these three locations," Cross said, pointing out the spots on a map he'd pulled up on his tablet.

"Over or under?"

He shook his head. "Neither. They skipped the weigh stations completely."

"Are they trying to get caught?"

"Maybe."

"Why?"

"So we can take the fall. It's not just meat those trucks are shipping, and you know it."

"Drugs?" I asked. It wouldn't be the first time.

"Why would that be beneficial?"

"I dunno, territory grab? Maybe they want to take a player off the board?"

"If we go down, so does the rest of the operation. Seems stupid to me. None of this works without us and our trucks."

"That's why I'm wondering if this has more to do with trying to hide something from us. From our guys."

"Fuck. This is getting out of hand. I mean, it's a lot of money, but when we don't know what's being transported . . ."

The shipping business was lucrative for a number of reasons, not the least of which was the protection our name offered our associates who needed to get their goods from point A to point B without any questions. Most of the time, these shipments ranged from weapons to live animals. Things that required excessive documentation, which didn't always suit the more unsavory sorts we dealt with. That's where we came in. But if someone had taken advantage of our business and was running something we hadn't approved . . . we couldn't let that slide.

"We've got to get to the bottom of this."

"What the hell do you think I've been trying to do? I'm not going on all these surveillance runs with Bishop for the fuck of it."

I sighed. "What do we do?"

"Keep squeezing the Russians. They're the biggest threat."

"Dom's been partnered with Twisted Cross since he took over. Why are they causing problems now?"

"We're weak, and they're making a play. Dad's gone, and everything's up in the air. I'm sure they know about River. We've got to show them we're stronger than ever, that she's not something they can use to get at us."

"They already pushed back." A phantom pain lanced my side, reminding me of their retaliation for us grounding them.

"I handled that."

That was news to me.

"When?"

"Last night."

I glanced around the spotless room, the acrid scent of bleach taking on a new meaning.

"Any loose ends?"

"Just one," Cross said with a heavy sigh.

I stayed silent, waiting him out.

"River caught me."

"How?"

"She found the passage."

"Jesus fuck, Cross. How much did she see?"

His jaw clenched, a muscle ticking as he ground his teeth. "Enough."

No wonder she wanted nothing to do with us. "You need to fix things with her. She hates us both right now, and it's not doing us any favors."

He snorted. "Like you did? Should I fuck her until she sees stars and try to hypnotize her with my dick?"

"No," I sneered, though the thought of knocking her up and tying her to me through a baby didn't seem like a bad idea. "But she needs a reason to remember she's on our side."

"I made sure she knew that if we go down, she's coming with us."

"That is not how you win over a girl like her, Cross. You need honey, not vinegar."

"What the fuck are you talking about?"

"What do we do when we get a skittish horse on this ranch? I know you haven't done much cowboying in the last few years, but surely you haven't forgotten everything." He didn't answer, so I kept talking. "We pet her real nice, say sweet things, talk to her in a soothing voice, and make sure she knows she can trust us. That's what we need to do with River. She's been broken and bruised by more than just you. Life's not been easy. You came in like a snorting bull, and she met you like a cornered barn cat. She knows she can't win, but she's gonna take out an eye while you ruin her."

"How is what you're proposing different from when I asked about hypnotizing her with my dick?"

I shook my head. "You're fuckin' stupid."

I had half a mind to tell him she'd loved him over me for decades, but he didn't deserve it. If he couldn't see how much he was giving up by treating her like dirt, I wasn't gonna enlighten him. River deserved to be cherished. None of what I'd told him was an act or a way to keep her out of things. I wanted to make her feel safe, make her trust me. Hell, I wanted to love her.

"She's going to the Cattleman's Gala. With or without us."

"What?" Cross's eyes snapped back to me.

"She RSVP'd on behalf of Cross Industries. Four tickets."

"Four?"

"Guess she plans on bringing a date."

My brother didn't have a response to that, but he was fuming. Seemed like a good time to kick him while he was down.

"She also signed you up for the silent auction."

"She what now?"

I didn't give him any more information. He could sweat it out a little. "If we're done here, I have an epic grovel to plan."

Cross shook his head, muttering as I headed for the ladder that would take me back to the stables.

"I'd brush up on your two-step if I were you, big bro. She looks like a dancer to me!" I called down the ladder.

The only answer I got was a grumbled, "Motherfucker."

twenty-two

River

I was mid-lipstick swipe when a knock sounded on my door. Thank God I checked my startle reflex in time, or I would have had a red streak across my cheek. No one wants to go to a gala filled with the richest of the rich looking like The Joker. Except maybe The Joker.

Brow furrowed, I tried to guess who it could be. Cross and I hadn't spoken since our showdown in the secret passage. I never got around to asking Bishop to be my date; I just couldn't reconcile myself to being the reason he was in an uncomfortable situation. Which only left one person...

"Leave me alone, Walker."

"It's me, siren." Bishop's voice was a low, rumbled rasp, and my thighs clenched in response.

I closed the tube of lipstick and strode to the door, pulling it open to reveal the man standing there, a navy blue three-piece suit hugging his big frame. He would fit right in with the wealthy cattlemen. Shiny cognac-colored boots and a cream Stetson pulled the look together.

I let out a low whistle. "Somebody cleans up nice."

He was too busy taking in my dress to acknowledge the compliment. I'd lucked out when I'd found the black floor-length number with a halter neck and thigh-high slit. It was sexy, understated, and stupidly expensive. In a word, it was perfect.

"I think that somebody is you." His stare burned into mine.

"Oh, this old thing?" I twirled, the skirt of my gown flaring out in a wave of silk.

"You ready to go?"

"Are you . . . driving us or something?"

He glanced down at the floor, then back up. "I might've overheard Walker complaining about you being too stubborn to let anyone escort you tonight. Thought I'd take a chance and see if you'd allow me on your arm."

It might have been the most words he'd said to me in a single go. He wasn't the chattiest man, but whew, was he potent.

"I wanted to ask you, but I didn't want you to feel pressured."

I hadn't intended to admit that, but knowing what tonight might cost him, I felt he'd earned a bit of my vulnerability.

His answering smile, that soft, slow curl of his lips, had a bolt of heat flaring to life in my belly.

"I think I can handle it."

"You sure? That means touching."

He leaned in and whispered, "I just need to be the one in charge tonight, sweetheart."

I swallowed, mouth suddenly dry. "I don't have a problem with that."

He offered me his arm. "Then let's get this show on the road."

Slipping my fingers through the crook of his elbow, I was very aware of the slight tension that coiled at my touch. My eyes snapped up to his face, where I found the same to be true. His jaw tightened and his nostrils flared, and I felt how hard he was trying to move past the discomfort.

"We don't have to do this, Sterling. I can go on my own."

"The hell you will. If I can't do something as simple as dance with you, how can I keep you safe?"

"Safe from what?"

Steel gray eyes locked on mine. "Everything."

It felt like the air had been knocked from my lungs. I hadn't spent a whole lot of time with Bishop since the night he'd discovered the truth hidden in those manila envelopes. I'd forgotten how his presence made me feel like I'd stuck my finger in a light socket. The man was dangerous in the best possible sense of the word.

"Okay, if you're sure. But I'm gonna warn you, I like to dance."

"I used to. Before." I hated the shadow in his expression. I wanted to figure him out and help him heal.

"I haven't had a reason to let someone lead in a long time," I admitted. "Not since I left home. It seems like since then, the world's been out to get me, and there hasn't been time for something as silly as dancing."

A muscle feathered in his jaw before his entire body relaxed, and he gifted me with a rare smile. "How about tonight we just pretend there's nothing else in our way. It's you and me, and that's all that matters."

I swallowed past the lump in my throat and said, "Deal. Now take me out, cowboy. I bought this dress, and I want you to show me off."

He chuckled and led me out of the lodge to where the limo was waiting for us. Cross and Walker were already standing outside, impatience and something I couldn't quite put my finger on stamped on their handsome faces. They looked just as delicious as Bishop did in their black suits and matching hats. That's where the similarities ended, though. Cross opted for classic elegance while Walker chose opulence. He had velvet lapels to go with the subtle design in his jacket and silver tips on his boots. It was like looking at a panther and a peacock.

"Walker. Danny." I said, pointedly staring at each of them in turn.

Cross fumed as he opened the door for me. Even though his growl of displeasure made it clear he was annoyed, his southern manners wouldn't allow him to let me get the door myself. The thought of him having to watch me all night with Bishop bolstered my spirits. He should see exactly what kind of man I deserved. One who wanted to take care of me. Not one who broke me.

Or used me.

The reminder of their betrayal was enough to cool any appreciation I might have had for their appearance. Just because they were pretty to look at didn't make them good men. Or even tolerable ones, for that matter. After all, predators were always the most beautiful creatures. That was what made them so dangerous.

I decided then and there to do my best to ignore them for the rest of the evening. It was just Bishop and me tonight. As agreed. And that was just fine by me.

WE WERE SURROUNDED by a sea of silk, sequins, and cowboy hats. Oh, and don't forget the hairspray. I was thankful the doors to the gardens were open, or it would have been impossible to breathe without choking on it.

True to his word, Bishop had kept me close and danced with me for most of the evening. It had been damn near perfect, to be honest. Minus the awkward run-in with dear old Cecilia. The look on her face when I'd walked in with the Cross brothers had been priceless. But when she'd realized I was there with Bishop, she'd practically started rubbing herself against Cross like a bitch in heat. Not gonna lie; I enjoyed watching him sweat, especially when she led him over to the silent auction table and pointed out what could only be his entry.

"What are you grinning about?" Bishop whispered in my ear as he handed me a glass of champagne.

"Oh, nothing. Cross Industries is just very charitable this year, and I believe Junior just realized how generous we've been."

When Cross's gaze lasered in on me, I stiffened on instinct. He was pissed with a capital P.

Bishop's warm palm pressed against the small of my back, lips close to my ear as he said, "Let's take a walk. You need some air."

"I do?" I asked with a laugh, recognizing that this was just another way Bishop was protecting me.

"I'm told the flowers are mighty pretty. Let's go pick some."

I snorted at the ridiculous and utterly un-Bishop answer. I couldn't picture him holding a single flower, let alone a bouquet. Lies. I could. It was fucking hilarious.

"I don't think we're allowed to pick these. Pretty sure it's in the bylaws or something, but a walk sounds nice. The stars are out, and it's quiet."

"Exactly my point. C'mon, I want to get you alone for a minute. I'm tired of sharing you with every pair of eyes in this ballroom."

People had been looking our way, sure, but it wasn't me they were interested in. I'd caught several women eyeing my date like he was about to be their next meal. If they weren't careful, my claws would come out. Then there was Walker, smiling, flirting, and dancing with every pretty girl he could find, but never taking his attention off me for more than a few minutes at a time. He watched me like he could sense me slipping away.

I felt Cross's stare boring into my back the whole way out the side exit, but I forced myself not to give in and turn my head.

Bishop steered us to the left, his hand never leaving my back as he guided me to the far corner of the patio, well out of the way of the ballroom and its guests.

The air was crisp with the spicy bite of lavender roses from the well-maintained garden nearby. Combined with the canopy of twinkling stars and the music still flooding out the open doors, it felt like a scene from some kind of historical romance. If only I had a dashing gentleman who wanted to ruin me.

Oh, wait.

As if on cue, Bishop carefully tucked a stray curl behind my ear and then pressed his lips to the sensitive skin along the side of my neck. I shivered, my fingers twitching with the need to touch him. But I fisted my hands instead, not wanting to accidentally destroy the fragile bonds between us. He must have noticed my inner turmoil, because his rough whisper sounded in my ear.

"Behind your back, baby. No touching. That's my job."

Oh God. His deep voice slipped over me, like velvet and whiskey with just a hint of gravel. My pussy throbbed in response. I hadn't had what I'd consider very many adventurous partners. There'd been one guy who'd wanted to play with handcuffs, but he came about a minute after putting them on me, so I figured that didn't really count.

Something told me Bishop wasn't playing, though. The ease with which he maneuvered my body and growled his commands told me he knew exactly what he was doing.

I did as I was told, my eyes fluttering closed as his stubble scraped along my sensitive skin. "I shouldn't touch you, siren. It's against the rules."

"Fuck the rules."

Low laughter vibrated across my neck, and goosebumps

followed in its wake. "I wondered if you were a good girl or a bad one. I'll let you in on a secret."

"What?"

"I like them bad. It's much more fun that way."

His fingers slid along the exposed flesh of my thigh, running up, up, up the slit of this dress until he found my lace-covered cunt.

"Feels like you agree," he murmured before lifting his head and covering my mouth with his.

Kissing Bishop was a whole lot like drowning. My heart raced, my breath caught, and my mind went blissfully empty. Time froze, cocooning us both for one perfect moment, as his mouth moved against mine, claiming me in the most perfect way. Need coiled inside me, and I writhed against my hands, pressing them against the brick so I wouldn't accidentally break his rules. I had a feeling that wasn't the kind of bad girl he liked, and if I were to disobey him, I'd lose him just as fast.

"Spread your legs for me, siren," he rasped against my lips. "I need to feel how slick you are because of me."

My only response was a whimper as I did as he asked. It felt like I was seconds away from coming, and he hadn't even touched me yet.

"Bishop," I finally managed.

"No, baby. You call me Sterling. You're the only one who gets that name, and I want you to fucking use it." He slid his fingers past my panties and sank two inside me in a slow glide. "Especially when I'm inside you."

"Fuck, Sterling."

"Say it again," he ordered, curling those fingers and lighting me up.

"Sterling. God, it feels so good."

He let out a little rumble as he repeated the motion. I rocked against him, seeking more, and he chuckled. "You better be careful, siren. You're already dripping down my hand. You should probably move your skirt to the side unless you want to ruin the silk and have everyone inside know exactly what we were up to out here. Because I'm making you come all over my fingers no matter what."

Who was this man, and what had he done with my strong, silent giant?

"Personally, I don't care who knows. I'd eat you out in the middle of the goddamn dance floor so long as you screamed my name when you came."

Again, who the fuck was this? I really liked this side of him.

"Jesus. Your mouth."

"What about it?"

"It's dirty."

"Not yet. We'll save that for when I can get you on your back with your legs spread wide for me." He brushed his thumb over my clit faster and faster until I was shaking with the need to come. "Hurry up, siren. Someone's coming. I'd much rather get you off before I get caught with my hand in the cookie jar."

I thought I heard footsteps, and panic clawed at me, but Bishop held me in place and worked me harder.

"Eyes on me. I want to watch you fall apart."

I tried, I really did, but the heat burning in his gaze was too much. That, along with the threat of being discovered, had me teetering on the brink.

"Kiss me. I'm going to scream." I was so close. So fucking close. "Please."

He did, his tongue spearing my lips and sending me over the edge into pleasure. I whimpered against him, but he swallowed most of my moans as I clamped down, milking his fingers like they were his cock.

"Fuck, that was beautiful," he said against my lips before he pulled his fingers free of me.

Then he pushed them into my mouth, making me suck them clean of my own orgasm. No one had ever done that before, made me taste myself, and a fresh wave of desire rose within me.

His lips chased his fingers, tasting me as our tongues tangled together.

"So fucking good. Next time you can clean it off my lips."

God.

Wanting to do to him what he'd done to me, I rasped, "Or your cock?"

His lips curled in that dangerous smirk. "Careful what you wish for, siren. Cause I'll fucking give it to you."

twenty-three

...

Cross

"So that's the new head honcho, huh?" Brett Ransom said as he took up space next to me, whiskey on his breath and the lingering scent of a cigar on his suit.

"Yep." I didn't bother looking up as I scrawled an obscene amount of money beside River's name on the silent auction bid. If she thought she was going to make me miserable, she was wrong.

Two can play that game, sparrow.

Pleased with myself, I picked up my whiskey.

"She giving you boys trouble?"

"Yep."

I knocked back my drink and caught the eye of a passing cocktail waitress. I didn't have to say a damn thing. She snatched my glass and gave me a saucy wink. I'd have a new one in minutes.

"At least she's easy on the eyes. It can't be all bad if you have a pretty little thing like her traipsing around the ranch."

My jaw clamped tight as I bit back the threat on the tip of my tongue. "Wouldn't know. I don't do any looking."

"Well, that's a damn shame. Woman like that deserves to

be appreciated." Calculating eyes slid my way. "That mean she's available?"

"No," Walker answered as he joined us. "Definitely not. She's off-limits."

Brett smirked. "I see."

You don't see shit, you rodeo clown.

"That's interesting."

I followed his gaze to where River was being escorted outside by Bishop, the cowboy's hand resting just over the swell of her ass.

He continued spouting his shit. "Seems to me she's only got eyes for your ranch hand. I woulda thought one of you boys'd stake a claim by now. Mighty risky to let her get away. You never know who might come sniffing around. But I suppose it's better one of your own than . . ."

My blood ran cold as Bishop and River passed, and beyond them, I caught sight of Dominik Volkov, staring her down like a hungry shark. The Russian boss was seated in the corner, of course, worried someone was gonna shoot him in the back. I didn't blame him. I would if I could.

"He's got her in his sights, Cross. Everyone knows she's holding you both by your balls. I'd tread carefully if I were you."

"You don't know shit, Ransom."

His eyebrows lifted over amused brown eyes. "I know that man has a reputation with the ladies. He won't hesitate to wine and dine your girl if he thinks it will get one up on you. A woman like her, with the power and money she now possesses? That's a prize, gentlemen. You should do something to ensure you're the ones who win it." He gave us a silent cheers and finished his drink. "Now if you'll excuse me, I need to see about finding a prize of my own."

"You think he's right?" Walker asked, taking Ransom's spot next to me. "Is Dom seducing our girl a real threat?"

I wanted to say no, but I sure as shit hadn't given her

reason to stay away from other men. I'd practically thrown her at them. "I wouldn't put it past him. Ransom didn't say it, but it was pretty damn clear. All Volkov has to do is sweep her off her feet and marry her. Then he'll take everything we have. We won't have to worry about her leaving and Cross Industries going up for auction. He'll fuck us over while he's fucking her."

Walker went uncharacteristically silent, his attention trained on the table where Dom sat. We both knew everything I'd said was true. Subterfuge was much less messy than an out-and-out war. And Dom hadn't become the boss by making stupid moves. If he could weasel his way into River's heart, we'd be fucked in more ways than one. The idea of her with him made my skin crawl.

In a lot of ways, he and I were the same. At least on paper. He was rich. He was good-looking, that blond hair and icy blue stare always getting him attention from the ladies. Motherfucker could be charming when he wanted to be. Having an accent didn't hurt; that always seemed to make women melt. Add to that the fact he was under forty, had inherited his uncle's empire, and had the brains and ruthlessness to double it in two years, and the man was a catch for any woman. What they didn't see was the reality behind the facade. His hands were soaked in the blood of countless victims, and his empire was built on a mountain of their corpses.

Fuck.

As if he knew my thoughts, Dom glanced across the ballroom and locked eyes with me. His mouth curled up in a threatening grin as he raised his glass in a mock toast.

The man stood, drink in hand, focus now trained in the direction River'd gone before he followed.

She'll be okay. She's with Bishop. He won't let anything happen to her.

Even though I told myself Bishop would keep her safe, I couldn't shake the feeling I was wrong. Volkov had already made it clear he was coming for me, and he was a cutthroat and devious monster. Once he set his sights on something, there was no stopping him. He wasn't exactly the kind of guy to follow a moral code. Not even a skewed one.

For the first time I could remember, icy fear worked its way into my veins.

River may never be mine, but I'd be damned before I'd let that Russian bastard try and take her from me.

He'd use her up and throw her away once he got what he wanted.

"Don't worry, brother. He's not going to touch her. I'll make sure of it." Walker's voice was cold and calculated. Right now he wasn't my carefree, reckless little brother. He was a soldier preparing his battle strategy.

"How do you plan to do that?"

"Fucker can't marry her if I do it first."

That made my heart lurch. Walker wanted to *marry* River? Why did the thought twist my stomach into a knot?

"She'll never agree to that."

"I think you underestimate the power of a good grovel."

"I think you underestimate her ability to hold a grudge."

Walker snorted. "That's where you and I are wildly different, Cross. I'm not afraid to let her put me on my knees. Give me some credit. The good lord didn't bless me with these looks for nothing. I'll have a fiancée and be working on an heir inside a week."

"You're fucking deluded."

"No. I'm fucking in love."

twenty-four
...
Bishop

 could still feel echoes of her cunt fluttering around my fingers as she righted her dress. Her cheeks were flushed from the orgasm I'd just given her, and the scent of her arousal was all over me. I hated that we had to go back to the party. That I couldn't toss her over my shoulder and take her to my bed. I wanted her bound and pliant. Ready for me to sink deep inside her and make her scream again.

"You keep making those sweet little whimpers, siren, and I'm gonna lose sight of why I can't sink inside you right here."

"Why can't you?"

This woman was fucking trouble. She made me forget the real reason I was here. How much danger I put her in just by getting close to her.

She's already in danger. Cross saw to that.

"Believe me, I want to. I want nothing more than to see my cum dripping down your thighs and know you're mine. But something tells me that won't go over well with this crowd. You're on everyone's radar tonight, and not just because you're so fucking stunning."

Her eyes were hooded as she swallowed, and I resisted

the urge to collar her throat with my hand. She was bringing out every dark urge I had, the ones I'd long thought buried. I didn't just want to fuck this woman, I wanted to own her. Completely.

That thought, more than any other, terrified me.

I was too broken.

She'd never want me if she knew the truth about my past. About the things I'd done.

My scars.

I shuddered, pushing away from her and stiffening as I caught a hint of cigar smoke in the night air. We weren't alone. I'd been so wrapped up in her that I'd gotten fucking sloppy.

"Get behind me and stay there, siren."

"What are y—"

"Don't argue." I turned to face the figure in the distance, putting my body in front of hers, completely shielding her. Out of habit, I also performed a quick mental check of my weapons, making sure they were still in place. "Make yourself presentable for polite company, pretty girl. We have to get back. You've got people waiting on you."

I could sense her confusion and the flicker of hurt my abrupt shift had caused. It made me feel like a bastard, but only for a second. I'd rather her think me an ass than let someone sneak up on us in a vulnerable moment.

Offering her my arm, I kept her as far away from our observer as possible, my attention tuned in to his movements while I led her toward the doors.

"Does Cross know you're plucking his sweet little bird?" Dominik Volkov said, his voice wholly unwelcome.

What the fuck is he doing here? The Russian crime lord rarely went anywhere without an army of sycophants to shield him. He was as elusive as a damn ghost, yet here he was. Alone. In the middle of a fancy party for ranchers, of all places. That could only mean one thing. He was making a play. A big one.

Fuck.

I had to get her out of here. But before I could do anything, River stiffened in my arms. But not from fear. Anger poured out of her as she twisted around and snapped back.

"Excuse me? Do you see a fucking cage? I am no one's anything."

"A gilded cage is still a cage . . . *sparrow*."

"Who the fuck are you?"

Dom pushed off the wall and sauntered up to us. I instinctively moved in front of River, but the stubborn woman wasn't having it. She slipped past me and got right in the Russian mob boss's face. My hand went to my gun, ready to take the asshole down if he so much as touched her.

He smirked and let out a patronizing laugh. "My mistake. Such fire in you. I see you aren't a sparrow after all. That's good. I prefer a phoenix. Rare and beautiful, even in their destruction."

She huffed. "You forgot fictional."

"You're going to be fun, aren't you, Ms. Adams?"

He reached out as though he was going to brush a lock of hair away from her face, but I snagged her by the elbow and tugged her against me. "We'd best be going. Cross will be looking for you."

"It was a pleasure meeting you, Phoenix."

"Pity I can't say the same," she said through a fake-ass smile.

I pulled her away without saying anything. And Volkov remained silent only long enough to let us take two steps before his voice floated after us.

"See you around . . . Special Agent Bishop."

Static filled my ears as everything around me slowed. I'd already picked an escape route and was calculating how long it would take us to get clear of the garden before someone came out and discovered his body when I spun back around, hand reaching into my jacket for my gun.

But the bastard was gone. We didn't refer to him as a ghost for nothing.

"Special Agent?" River whispered.

"You need to forget you heard that."

"Sterling, what did he mean? Don't lie to me."

Before we returned to the ballroom, I pushed her into a darkened corner and got in her face, needing her to understand how imperative it was she keep my secret. Her life quite literally depended on it. Not even I could keep her safe if she let it slip in the wrong company.

If Cross didn't kill her, my people would. We were too close to breaking this case wide open. They might be the good guys, but there was no way they'd allow a woman to ruin years of undercover work. What was one more body in the grand scheme of things?

For the greater good was the only mantra that mattered, and it excused all manner of sins. I knew that better than anyone.

"I can't promise I'll never keep things from you, River. My life is filled with secrets, and there's nothing I can do about it. But there are some things it's safer for you not to know, and this is one of them. Stay away from him. He's dangerous and will use you to get to Cross."

"I don't matter to Cross. He wouldn't give a damn." The hurt in her voice echoed in her eyes, and all I wanted to do was reassure her that she was worth everything.

"That's where you're wrong." I backed away from her and sighed. "Now come on, we need to get inside. I'm sure you're missed."

She stopped me before heading inside with a featherlight touch. It took everything in me not to flinch. "Just tell me one thing, Sterling."

A sharp nod was all I gave her.

"Are you in danger?"

The answer to that wasn't one she really wanted. The fact that she asked told me she already knew it anyway. So instead of making her worry, I decided to reassure her instead.

"Siren, I *am* the danger."

twenty-five

...

River

$\mathcal{T}$he man who invented high heels was surely a sadist. He had to be. And there was no way it was a woman, because these shoes were beautiful but cruel torture devices. I slipped out of the sky-high stilettos and opened my door with an almost indecent groan.

Tonight hadn't gone as I'd expected. That's not even taking into account the mind-blowing orgasm I'd experienced at the tips of Sterling's talented fingers. Jesus, who knew the man had been hiding that filthy mouth behind all those smoldering stares? He was the one bright spot in an otherwise shitty situation. A shit-uation, if you will.

I tossed my shoes in the corner of the room, then reached behind my back and unzipped the silk gown Sterling had completely ruined. There would be no saving this fabric, not with the way he'd made me come. I'd somehow managed to finish out the night without sitting and leaving a wet spot on the back of the fabric, but once I got in the car to head home, there was nothing to be done. You'd think things would have *cleared up* by then, but no. The man had made me fucking gush. And every time he looked my way, my body reacted as though his hands were on me.

It was obscene.

I'd be embarrassed if I wasn't so eager to do it again.

I let the fabric fall to the floor and turned to my bed with a sigh, contemplating whether I was going to risk going to sleep with a full face of makeup and no PJs when my eyes snagged on the carefully arranged presents sitting next to my pillow.

Walker.

I knew they were from him without having to inspect the eclectic offering. He'd been watching me like a wounded puppy all night, and I'd had to force myself not to be swayed by him.

This must be what he'd meant by a big gesture.

I hesitated before moving to the side of the bed, not sure if I wanted to give him the chance to wear me down with thoughtful gifts. But in the end, I was too curious not to see what constituted a proper grovel in his mind.

The first thing that drew my eye was a bouquet of my favorite flowers, Queen of the Night tulips. Twenty-four of them were bundled together, the stems wrapped in paper and tied with a black ribbon. Nestled within the blooms was a notecard, Walker's familiar scrawl across the front.

PLEASE READ ME.

I sighed but reached for the card, opening the envelope and pulling it free.

> **LADYBUG,**
>
> **I KNOW I MESSED UP AND BROKE WHAT WE HAD, BUT I ALSO KNOW YOU ARE WORTH FIGHTING FOR. SO CONSIDER ME ALL IN ON US.**
>
> **IF YOU THINK I'M NOT WORTH IT, ALLOW ME TO REMIND YOU WHY FALLING IN LOVE WITH YOUR BEST FRIEND IS THE MOST PERFECT WAY TO DO IT.**
>
> **EXAMPLE ONE: I'LL ALWAYS REMEMBER YOUR FAVORITE FLOWER, AND I'LL DO ANYTHING TO GET IT FOR YOU JUST TO SEE YOU SMILE.**
>
> **SOMETHING TELLS ME THAT'S NOT ENOUGH FOR YOU TO TRUST ME AGAIN, SO MOVE ON TO THE NEXT GIFT IF YOU NEED MORE CONVINCING.**
>
> **ALWAYS YOURS,**
> **WALKER**

My heart was already questioning everything my brain had decided we were going to do. Fucking Walker, knowing exactly how to get to me.

I reached for the sweets next, laughing a little at the nearly five-pound bag of orange Starburst, all already unwrapped. It had been our favorite candy as a kid, and Walker and I had always fought about who got the orange ones. Whenever we fought, he'd always apologize by offering me the last orange Starburst. Or, if we weren't together, he'd leave one for me on my pillow to let me know he was sorry and all was forgiven. I guess it was our version of a white flag.

> **I THOUGHT YOU COULD USE A LITTLE SOMETHING TO HELP SWEETEN UP YOUR FEELINGS TOWARD ME. IT**

> **WAS HARD TO GIVE ALL THESE UP, BUT I'LL GIVE YOU EVERYTHING IF I GET YOU IN RETURN.**

Against my better judgment, I softened toward him. A small grin twisted my lips as I took out one piece of candy and popped the tart square into my mouth. The man was a genius at seduction, but I already knew that. Such a simple set of things, my favorite flowers and candy, and I was already putty in his hands. I'd been lying to myself when I said I'd never let him in again.

He hadn't stopped there, though. The cherry on top of this Walker Cross sundae was a neatly folded Twisted Cross Ranch T-shirt. I was pretty sure the shirt itself wasn't the gift, because as soon as I picked it up, the spicy scent of his cologne hit my nose.

The note fell to the bed as I slid the cool cotton over my head.

> **SINCE YOU AREN'T READY TO LET ME HOLD YOU, I FIGURED I'D WRAP YOU UP IN ME IN A DIFFERENT WAY. IMAGINE THOSE ARE MY ARMS HOLDING YOU TIGHT, PRESSING YOU INTO ME AS YOU DRIFT OFF TO SLEEP. I WISH THINGS WERE DIFFERENT AND THAT I'D NEVER FUCKED THIS UP IN THE FIRST PLACE, BUT I'LL SLEEP BETTER KNOWING I'M WITH YOU SOMEHOW.**
>
> **I LOVE YOU, RIVER. NO MATTER WHAT YOU THINK OF ME. AND NO MATTER HOW LONG IT TAKES, I'LL GET YOU TO SEE THAT YOU LOVE ME TOO. WE BELONG TOGETHER, DARLIN'. ALWAYS HAVE. ALWAYS WILL.**
>
> **I'M NOT LETTING YOU GO AGAIN. EVER.**
>
> **— W**

Goddammit. Tears sprang to my eyes. I hated crying. I hated that Walker Cross had me even close to crying and feeling bad for sticking to my guns. But if I was being honest with myself, the moment I cut him off, I'd already begun to yearn for him.

I sat down hard on the bed, frustration making my eyes burn as I fought off the tears. I'd cried more since arriving at this damn ranch than I had in years. I was not this girl. The mopey pining for a man to love her girl.

I'd been that girl ten years ago when Cross fucked me and abandoned me with nothing. The last thing I wanted was to be her again, especially not over another Cross boy. But it was hard to think of Walker as my enemy. He'd never been anything other than kind and caring. He always treated me like I was special to him, even when we were gangly preteens. Was he sincere now?

My gaze flicked to the ruined dress on the floor, and flashes of heat raced over my skin as memories of what Bishop had just done to me tonight took hold. How could I be crying over one man while still riding the high of another's touch? On paper, Bishop was the obvious choice for me. We didn't have a twisted past, he hadn't done anything to hurt or mislead me, and we clearly had chemistry. But maybe that was only because there was still so much about him I didn't know. He'd admitted he had secrets, things he could never tell me. I mean, he was a damn government agent, for crying out loud. The man was as complicated as the Cross brothers, messy history or not.

Did Bishop know how deep the bodies were buried on this ranch? Did I? A chilling thought worked its way to the forefront of my mind. Cross murdered the man who'd attacked Walker. He shot and killed him; I had no doubt. The fact that I hadn't told a soul made me an accessory. Would Bishop turn us all in? Would he sacrifice me for the sake of his job? And more to the point, was it really so bad when Cross was avenging his brother?

What did it say about me and my own skewed set of morals that I didn't blame him for what he'd done? Growing up with Bear as my guardian had taught me that love was shades of gray in a justice system that was black and white. He was the kind of guy who would burn the world down for the people he loved. He'd taught me to be the same. I wanted nothing less from my partners. Partner. Fuck.

Cross proved he was the same, and I couldn't fault him for that. Which meant only one thing. Bishop could never know what I'd seen. I wouldn't send Cross to prison for something I'd have done myself if given the chance.

God, my stupid heart was a disaster. She craved them all. Even the one man I'd sworn to hate for the rest of my days. The one I used to believe was my dream come true when, in actuality, he was more of a nightmare. A monster hiding in plain sight.

I came to Twisted Cross Ranch hoping to uncover the truth of how my parents died. To get some closure and move on. Instead, I'd become wrapped in the Cross family's web of lies and deceit while somehow also tangling myself up with three men I couldn't choose between.

As if on cue, an email notification dinged on my phone, pulling me away from thoughts of the three men I wanted.

To: River@RAdamsCPA.com
From: an0nym0us@protonmail.com
Subject: It's not over

They've got you in their sights.

Just below the cryptic message were two images side by side. The first was my parents dressed to the nines and slow dancing. The Cattleman's banner in the background proclaiming it was the same event I'd attended tonight, just a decade earlier. The second image was me, taken tonight while I'd been dancing with Bishop. The expression on my face was near identical to my mother's.

It was eerie seeing myself in such a similar position. Or perhaps that was because of the red X scribbled across my face.

Under the photos was one final line of text, and it sent a chill through me.

The clock's ticking, River.

twenty-six

Walker

The morning after the gala, I'd hoped to see River in the kitchen for coffee, or maybe poolside as she swam laps. I hadn't. In fact, I hadn't heard a peep from her and was starting to worry she'd never gotten the gifts I'd left her. Or maybe she had and just thought I was the world's biggest sucker.

Maybe she'd run off with Bishop and was halfway to Vegas.

Nope. We are not manifesting that shit, Walker. Or whatever the hell those woo-woo types call it. Positive thoughts only. By the end of today, she'll have your ring on her finger.

I couldn't let my girl slip away because of something stupid like a misunderstanding. Striding toward her bedroom, I peeked in, hoping to catch her so we could talk. All I found was a neatly made bed and the lingering sweetness of her perfume. Where had she gone? More importantly, what could she be up to?

If Cross was to be believed, she was off trying to dig up our skeletons. But he didn't know her like I did. River wasn't trying to ruin us; she just wanted out of a situation she never asked for. She wasn't the kind of person who would go out of her way to tear us down just to make herself feel better. In short, she wasn't like us.

River Adams had always been too good for the likes of me, but she made me want to be better, be the kind of man she deserved. I could do that for her.

Determination burning bright inside me, I left her room and headed for the one place in this house I hadn't entered in years. Not since Mama died. My hand shook as I reached for the door, memories of her sitting at her vanity as she put on her earrings for a night out with Dad flooding me. I'd been little when she died, so my recollections were sparse, but the way she'd smile at me was permanently etched into my mind. When my father made me feel unwanted, she was the one who taught me about unconditional love. She was the only reason for the good parts about me.

Realizing I was still hovering outside the door like a loser, I took a deep breath and opened it, quickly darting inside. With my luck, Cross would choose this exact moment to walk down the hall, and I didn't want him to try and talk me out of anything, so I made sure the door was shut behind me before I took in my surroundings.

It was a time capsule dedicated to Mama. Even though Dad had never stopped using this room, nothing had changed. Her silk robe hung from the back of a chair, and a bottle of perfume still sat next to her jewelry box on the dresser. A pair of diamond studs glittered from the small container on the vanity table as I flicked on the light. It felt like he'd just been waiting for her to come back.

Overwhelming grief slammed into me for just a second. She'd never know the woman I loved, the family I'd have one day, hell, she'd never really know me. It's what made this moment even more meaningful for me. In a lot of ways, it sort of felt like I had her approval. Like she was watching over me and guided me here so she could be part of such a life-changing event.

I moved until I was at her dresser, hands resting on her jewelry box.

"You'd have loved River, Mama. Casey and Elsie's little girl, remember? I think she was just a baby, but I'm sure you got to meet her. She's perfect for me. I don't think you could've chosen anyone better. She doesn't put up with my shit. And she's the prettiest girl I've ever known. I want to marry her, and I want to give her your ring. I know Cross is supposed to get it, but the only woman who deserves to wear it is River."

Maybe it was stupid, talking to the ghost of a woman who'd long since passed, but it made me feel closer to her.

I lifted the lid and pulled out the two-and-a-half-carat cushion-cut pink diamond with a diamond-encrusted platinum band. Senior may have been an asshole, but he had taste, and he loved my Mama. The ring was still pristine, nestled in its velvet box along with the matching wedding and anniversary bands. I'd save those for later. Right now, I needed to get the engagement part handled.

I was taking a risk by asking River to be mine, but a big part of me knew it was right. I may have only come up with the idea last night, but I'd known in my heart since I was a kid that she would be the one to take my name. Our circumstances had just given me the perfect opportunity. We were meant to be together; there'd just always been a Cross-shaped obstacle in my way. Not anymore.

Pocketing the ring, I pressed a kiss to my fingertips before laying them on the framed picture of Mama that sat on the dresser. She'd been in her housecoat, hair a mess, exhausted, and cradling me as a newborn in a rocking chair. Cross was next to her, looking at her with such a sweet expression I almost couldn't tell it was him.

"Love you, Mama. I'm sorry I haven't come by to visit. I'll do better. I promise."

I gave the room one final look before shutting the door

and heading back toward the main part of the house. The sound of voices reached me, and I took it as a positive sign that one of them was the woman I'd been trying to track down all morning.

It was now or never. I'd never make it if this diamond had to burn a hole in my pocket for long. I wasn't a patient man. Hard to believe, I know.

"Okay, Walker. Time to make her yours," I said under my breath.

Before I could start down the stairs, my phone rang. I pulled it out, intending to send the caller to voicemail, but when I caught sight of McCreedy's name, I answered. As soon as my mind was made up about marrying River, I called our lawyer and asked him to apply for a marriage license.

"Is it done?" I asked by way of greeting.

"Not exactly."

"What the fuck does that mean?"

"You can't marry her, Walker."

"The hell I can't. There's nothing stopping me."

"Yes, there is. Her husband."

"What did you just say?"

"Your girl's already married."

"To who?" I snarled, ready to make her a fucking widow.

"Your brother."

To be continued.

Don't worry darlin' we won't leave you hangin'...for long.
Corruptor's Claim is coming Sept 2023.
Order your copy now!

more by meg & kim

<u>Twisted Cross Ranch</u>
A dark contemporary cowboy reverse harem

Sinner's Secret

Corruptor's Claim

Deadly Debt

the mate games universe

By K. Loraine & Meg Anne

WAR

OBSESSION

REJECTION

POSSESSION

TEMPTATION

PESTILENCE

PROMISED TO THE NIGHT (PREQUEL NOVELLA)

DEAL WITH THE DEMON

CLAIMED BY THE SHIFTERS

CAPTIVE OF THE NIGHT

LOST TO THE MOON

DEATH

HAUNTING BEAUTY

HUNTED BEAST

HATEFUL PRINCE

HEARTLESS VILLAIN

also by meg anne

BROTHERHOOD OF THE GUARDIANS/NOVASGARD VIKINGS

<u>UNDERCOVER MAGIC</u> (NORD & LINA)
A SEXY & SUSPENSEFUL FATED MATES PNR
HINT OF DANGER
FACE OF DANGER
WORLD OF DANGER
PROMISE OF DANGER
CALL OF DANGER
BOUND BY DANGER (QUINN & FINLEY)

THE CHOSEN UNIVERSE

<u>THE CHOSEN</u>
A FATED MATES HIGH FANTASY ROMANCE
MOTHER OF SHADOWS
REIGN OF ASH
CROWN OF EMBERS
QUEEN OF LIGHT
THE CHOSEN BOXSET #1
THE CHOSEN BOXSET #2

<u>THE KEEPERS</u>
A GUARDIAN/WARD HIGH FANTASY ROMANCE

The Dreamer (A Keeper's Prequel)

The Keepers Legacy

The Keepers Retribution

The Keepers Vow

The Keepers Boxset

The Forsaken

A Rejected Mates/Enemies-To-Lovers Romantasy

Prisoner of Steel & Shadow

Queen of Whispers & Mist

Court of Death & Dreams

Prince of Sea & Stars

A Standalone MMF Romantasy Adventure

Gypsy's Curse

A Psychic/Detective Star-Crossed Lovers UF Romance

Visions Of Death

Visions Of Vengeance

Visions Of Triumph

The Gypsy's Curse: The Complete Collection

also by k. loraine

THE BLACKTHORNE VAMPIRES
THE BLOOD TRILOGY
(CASHEL & OLIVIA)
Blood Captive

Blood Traitor

Blood Heir

BLACKTHORNE BLOODLINES
(LUCAS & BRIAR)
Midnight Prince

Midnight Hunger

THE WATCHER SERIES
Waking the Watcher

Denying the Watcher

Releasing the Watcher

THE SIREN COVEN
Eternal Desire (Shifter reluctant mates)

Cursed Heart (Hate to Lovers)

Broken Sword (MMF menage Arthurian)

STANDALONES

Cursed (MFM Sleeping Beauty Retelling)

REVERSE HAREM STANDALONES

Their Vampire Princess (A Reverse Harem Romance)

All the Queen's Men (A Fae Reverse Harem Romance)

about meg anne

USA Today and international bestselling paranormal and fantasy romance author Meg Anne has always had stories running on a loop in her head. They started off as daydreams about how the evil queen (aka Mom) had her slaving away doing chores, and more recently shifted into creating backgrounds about the people stuck beside her during rush hour. The stories have always been there; they were just waiting for her to tell them.

Like any true SoCal native, Meg enjoys staying inside curled up with a good book and her fur babies . . . or maybe that's just her. You can convince Meg to buy just about anything if it's covered in glitter or rhinestones, or make her laugh by sharing your favorite bad joke. She also accepts bribes in the form of baked goods and Mexican food.

Meg is best known for her leading men #MenbyMeg, her inevitable cliffhangers, and making her readers laugh out loud, all of which started with the bestselling Chosen series.

about k. loraine

USA Today Bestselling author Kim Loraine writes steamy contemporary and sexy paranormal romance. **You'll find her paranormal romances written under the name K. Loraine and her contemporaries as Kim Loraine.** Don't worry, you'll get the same level of swoon-worthy heroes, sassy heroines, and an eventual HEA.

When not writing, she's busy herding cats (raising kids), trying to keep her house sort of clean, and dreaming up ways for fictional couples to meet.

Made in United States
Orlando, FL
10 August 2024